JENNIFER

JENNIFER

A Boy, a Girl, and a Terrible Tragedy

ROBERT MITCHELL

authorHOUSE®

AuthorHouse™
1663 Liberty Drive
Bloomington, IN 47403
www.authorhouse.com
Phone: 1-800-839-8640

Published by AuthorHouse   08/24/2012

ISBN: 978-1-4772-2682-7 (sc)
ISBN: 978-1-4772-2675-9 (hc)
ISBN: 978-1-4772-2683-4 (e)

POEM

There was a young writer called George
who fell in love oh so young
he kept all this to himself
on a shelf
until he discovered by chance the one
who inspired his ideas
his thoughts
inspiration
a myth
a cloud
a phantomisation

He ran
he fell
stood up
ran again
his memories driving him almost insane
. . . this phantom so real
and yet in a haze
had the power to set his ardour ablaze
but then he discovered
she was nothing at all
an imaginary shadow
on a shadowy wall

He walks and he breathes and he thinks he's insane
as he imagines his phantom again and again
and then he returns
to his books on the shelf
and picks up the book
that he wrote by himself
and he cannot decide what is real and what's not
if he had what he had
or if he had not!!!

ACKNOWLEDGEMENTS

To my lovely wife Sue whose patience and love never cease to amaze me. To the girl's at the school without their characters this book could not have been written including the auburn haired girl who took a shine to me at a very early age and is the inspiration behind the book.

ABOUT THE BOOK

George's family were working class, moving from one tied cottage to another, which eventually took them to a Private girl's school.

George was still pining for his childhood sweetheart, who drowned in a boating accident along with her family.

A chance meeting with a new pupil at the school, Jennifer, helped him close that chapter in his life.

There now followed a warning from the past, schoolboy/ girl romance, ghosts, and chilling music.

He had lost the love of his life and was now building a new relationship or was he.

PRÉCIS

As a boy, growing up at an all-girls' boarding school is as exciting as it sounds. Over one hundred well-educated, polite girls from well-to-do backgrounds in your field of vision every day of your adolescent life, is a boy's dream. It wasn't that difficult to learn to accept their constant teasing knowing that it was a real privilege to be the only boy living at the school. The answer to their boy-baiting was never to show you were embarrassed or shocked by their antics. You had to learn fast and grow up fast, for these bright young ladies were looking for a chink in your armour to exploit.

The author lived at one such school in West Sussex; therefore he has touched on some genuine personal experiences in this book. He was the son of the school gardener and made the mistake of falling in love with a very pretty girl but alas he knew from her presence at the school he would never be able to make her his own. Deep inside he knew that the day would come when they would both grow up and go their separate ways but . . . life is full of surprises!

CONTENTS

CHAPTER 1

Mother, Father, my sister Karen and I, George, were living in a perfectly good council house in Emsworth. I had made a lot of friends in the street, always in and out of each other's houses but when father was made redundant from the local mushroom factory (a job he detested anyway) he thought it was a good idea to return to the tied cottage system. This was not the best of ideas as we found out on quite a few occasions, both previously and in the future for if you lose your job you lose your home.

I was four and we were moving to an estate owned by a doctor in Emsworth. Father was responsible for keeping the massive lawn between the main house and the tennis courts up to the standard of a bowling green. He also had to maintain four large herbaceous borders that were on either side of the lawn and a large circular rose garden. These were amply fed when father mucked out the two horses stabled in the courtyard, which was situated on the west side of the main house, a Georgian mansion. Our house made up one side, with the hay loft, stables and tack room completing the square. With the onset of Autumn I helped clear the leaves from the driveway to the main house as only a four year old boy could do, kicking them around and throwing them in the air.

Doctor Caine was a jovial man, quite tall, with dark hair and a beard; he always had time to spare when talking to Karen and myself and never left our company without parting with whatever change he had on him which was usually a two shilling piece each. I could not say the same for Mrs Caine who would scold him for parting with money during a recession.

Sadly I found out what the word recession meant as father was sacked. Our house was going to be converted into more stables so Mrs Caine could open a riding school, bringing in much needed revenue. As gardeners were queuing for work, cheaper labour could be used without housing them. Mother pleaded with father to apply for council accommodation again, but father seemed to be searching for something, for some reason he wanted to remain in the tied cottage system.

Our next move took us to a lovely house in Andover, our first semi detached, overlooking rolling hills as far as the eye could see. It was bliss, for me at least. I cannot say as much for Karen, for when we were invited next door to meet our only neighbours, their Labrador sunk his teeth into her arm. It must have looked more of a meal than the bone she was trying to give him, but then unfortunately there followed the agony of discovering she was allergic to penicillin, her head began to swell and I would say she was not having the best of times.

She didn't give up that easily in her quest for pain. We were discovering more about where we lived when we came across father. He was working in an inspection pit with a lorry over the top of it. The pit was kept a secret from us for obvious reasons, but we found it all the same. It took Karen all of a couple of minutes to lean over to say hello to father and fall in leaving her needing six stitches to a head wound.

Father was working for a man who drove one of the first Cougar sports cars. This poor man was driving home one night when a lorry pulled out from a side road leaving him with no room to manoeuvre. He hit the side of the lorry and died instantly. I overheard father telling mother the boss was dead, a few days later we were on the move again, which only lasted a month.

The new house was damp and smelly, not only that but we soon found out our garden was a shortcut for men with shotguns. When father remonstrated with them they explained the other route would take them hours to get to their shoot, if they could not use the shortcut. As a thank you for father letting them use the garden, rabbits and pheasants would be tied to our apple tree.

That was enough for mother; she couldn't stay a minute longer. We moved to a market garden/farm on the edge of the New Forest and lived in a flat above some disused stables. It was a working farm. Well some of it worked, the old covered wagons that would not have looked out of place in a western were well past their prime but they were good to play on. The pig sty worked, I can vouch for that as my bedroom window opened out on it.

I had six weeks off of school with glandular fever, six hot weeks in bed next to a pig sty, and father often warned me not to swing the lead. You never spoke out of turn to father, he was an aggressive man and if you said the wrong thing a fist would appear an inch from your face followed by some threatening expletive. He was the perfect gent to everyone else; it seemed he hated his family. I could see his point to a degree, not the aggression, his parents were god-fearing Victorians who made him and his sisters kneel before them each night to say the lord's prayer, and his mother would beat his sisters if they came in late from an evening out. Perhaps he thought that was the way of the world.

Fortunately Karen and I both inherited our mother's loving nature; unless you put us together then the sparks would fly. The flat overlooked a large stony yard, which is where I learned to ride a bicycle. If ever there was an incentive to keep your balance it was the thought of falling off and cutting your knees on the stones, luckily I was a quick learner.

We lived in a valley and if a storm broke in the night it became trapped, the thunder and lightning would roll around the hills keeping everyone awake. In the morning we would traipse along the farm track for our bus to take us to school in Ringwood. It was fun listening to kids exaggerate what the lightning had done to their houses and somehow managed to overturn their Dad's car. Once, I said the lightening had struck our horse chestnut tree and had brought down a branch nearly the same size as the tree, they all laughed, but I was telling the truth.

On Sundays after homework and chores were done I would go fishing in the nearby river Avon. It was fast flowing and clear, and even if no fish were biting, watching the may flies flit around the cattle drinking in the river made a peaceful scene.

Whilst living there mother wanted me to meet her father, Grandfather Williams. He was in a nursing home in Southsea, where my mother's family lived. He was a kind man, when we shook hands I noticed my hand disappeared into his, they were more like giant paws, huge and hairy, and when he stood up he dwarfed everyone in the room. However he was a wreck, a Coldstream Guardsman shell-shocked from the Great War.

Following a nod from Grandfather which I wasn't supposed to see, mother and father left the room to get some tea and biscuits. I believe Grandfather could tell me some fantastic stories about his life especially about the war, although looking around his room you would hardly believe he had anything to say as his room was barren except for his bed, a small table and an easy chair.

"Come here son", he said.

"Don't be afraid of an old man like me, I won't hurt you, so you're my grandson are you?" he said as he put an arm around me.

"Will you tell me about the war Granddad?"

"One day, son, one day", he added tactfully. Then I remembered mother's words, about not to pester him for war stories. He continued.

"I want to tell you that you are being looked after, you have a guardian angel, and you're not to be afraid of this. My Company had a guardian angel at a place called Mons where we were fighting, and we were outnumbered against the Germans. I knew we would be safe because I sensed it, the same way I am sensing it now, but not for me, for you, don't be afraid, but I must warn you." He stopped talking as the door opened. "Ah", he said. "Here's mum and dad with the tea".

Later as we stood to leave, my mother, father and me, I realised that the only person who should have stood there was my father. My mother and I along with grandfather should not have existed. For my grandfather was found asleep at his post on the Western Front, and he should have faced a firing squad, no one knows why he didn't face the death penalty for such a 'heinous' offence. My grandfather told me. "Don't be afraid, but

I must warn you." But warn me against what? I had to visit him again to find out. Don't be afraid! I was leaving the home terrified by what he had told me. On our way home I tried to make sense of it but why would anyone want to protect me, I had a mother and father to do that. Sadly I had to put it down to the ramblings of a mentally ill and very old man.

I was six years old and had moved as many times, so it came as no surprise when I discovered we were on the move again. There were allegations of stealing being spread amongst the workers, some were sacked, others were arrested and although father had nothing to do with it, he didn't like the atmosphere all this was creating, so he put in his notice and once again no job—no home. To make matters worse as far as I was concerned, we were moving to a private girl's school.

Having a sister who is eighteen months older than me I knew all about girls and what a pain they were, to be precise an anal pain! We were packing for the move and arguing over storage boxes, as I had collected them from the local store I wanted the best ones. The argument soon turned into a fight, using, of all things knitting needles and soon I had four holes in my back with blood coming from them. Game over as Grandmother Williams walked in; oblivious to the fact we were trying to kill each other. She had brought presents for us, a doll for Karen and a matchbox car for me which soon made us forget that the other one existed.

Gran asked me in her calm gentle voice if I would be so kind as to fetch father. He could certainly make himself scarce when he wanted to; it took me ages to find him as there were so many places he could be, the vegetable fields, the green houses, tractor garage, lawn mower garage. At last I saw him leaving the estate manager's office; the company wanted him to stay, but father's mind was settled on moving.

The three adults shut themselves in the kitchen leaving Karen and I to listen against the door. There was a lot of mumbling followed by a loud "NO" from mother. A few minutes later they came into the living room, with mother in tears. Grandfather had died. I started crying as I loved the old man even though I had only seen him once. Now whatever he was going to warn me about, he had taken to his grave.

Father told us to leave the room and to continue packing our toys. My back was still feeling painful following the fight with Karen, now I was going to live my life next to hoards of them. I had already decided they were all going to be a bunch of snobs with their quick wit and sarcastic comments, said behind a hand over their mouth and of course knee high socks and straw boaters. Yes I was really going to love living at a girls' school.

Having got lost countless times our removal lorry entered the school by way of a driveway, there being a gatehouse on one side and an orchard on the other and then it was lined with horse chestnut trees. It was August, and raining heavily, otherwise I would have noticed the name of the school. Also the driveway was very dark as the trees were in full leaf; they created a canopy that blocked out what little daylight there was peering through the storm clouds.

After the orchard there were tennis courts on the right with no nets, maybe it was disused, and fields on the left. As we drove towards the school, which was actually a converted large country house rather than a purpose built school, the drive split left and right. We took the left fork passing some unlit dismal looking huts that looked more like Army Barracks, until finally we did a sweeping turn to the front of this great looking old house, it was massive. I saw a frail little old lady meet father at the main door, the sort of lady you would help across the road. She was dressed in a dark tweed suit, and wore her dark hair up in a bun. She handed him some keys.

I was to learn that this frail lady ran the school, she was the headmistress. She would be in charge of all the staff, the kitchen gardens, the general running of the place and securing places for girls from around the world, the list was endless. There was one job she would ask no one else to do, which was, just before dusk and when the girls were on term breaks, she would check every room of this grand, but empty creepy place, and make sure all the windows were fastened.

The gatehouse we passed on the way in was to be our home, but was in need of some modernisation, so where were we to live until then? Adjacent to the gatehouse was a bit of ground with a caravan on it, Karen and I didn't know whether to laugh or cry as we looked at our temporary home for the next year.

So this school was called 'Farthings'! This was a name I never wanted to see again as long as I lived, how bitterly I cried when I lost my soul mate. My nightmare at such a young age started when my family used to live in a village called Farthings, just outside of Portsmouth. Mother and father did not want to leave the place as they had got on so well with the family who owned a large eighteenth—century mansion. We lived in a tied cottage within the grounds, mother would go to the house and clean, whilst father looked after the gardens, they were elderly people, the sort I would call grandparents.

They moved away when their daughter and son-in-law, together with their children, were wiped-out in a yachting accident. The girl was about my age, give or take a few weeks and I remember how very close we were, spending most of our very young days together—well as much as two little children could. Mother said there was a bond between the two of us. The little girl would come running to me and comfort me if I hurt myself, and I would do the same to her. Neither of our mothers could ever work out why we were so close, in my dreams I would grow up with her, and may well have done so if it wasn't for that tragic day. How I cried night after night and never really came to terms with losing her, and now I was to be reminded of her every day at 'Farthings School for Girls'!

I went round to the gatehouse to see what needed modernising, the place was deserted, there was an old tin bath hanging on the outside wall next to the back door, and an outside loo. They both needed turning into a bathroom, and the kitchen with its earthen floor was to be demolished. Yes I thought, about a year in that damp, cramped caravan. Thank you father!

Whilst the 'girls' were away we started to investigate our new home and found that beyond the orchard was the kitchen garden, and further on was the school swimming pool, surrounded by some trees to the south and west. There was a field with some cows to the east; to the north was a rose garden and a massive lawn, then the main house. There was a courtyard with a clock tower over the entrance, with a working clock that struck the hour and although we lived at the bottom of the drive it still kept me awake at night. I wonder how the girls fared!!

Our caravan home was dreadful, it was cramped and we could all see that a great deal of toleration was going to be required whilst living there. To make matters a whole lot worse Karen caught pneumonia, which for a while was touch and go. It was during this time I became very close to her for I had lost my little female friend at the previous place called Farthings; I didn't want to lose my sister as well.

Mother booked us into a school in one of the surrounding villages, suddenly I had a new name given to me by my class mates, 'Mitch', the name stayed with me for my entire school life no matter which school it was. There were some vindictive kids at school, all from the local council estate and when they found out we lived in a caravan we were called gypsies. This seemed to bother these kids more than it did me or Karen, when they saw they were making fools of themselves they left us alone.

I became very guarded about the girls' school. If I went to any of my friends' houses and found they had an older brother who was showing too much of an interest in where I lived, that friend became an ex-friend. Sorry girls.

It was 1961 and the summer holidays were here. As we had lived in the caravan for almost a year father was going to treat us to a holiday, a camping holiday, in a tent, great, to be fair to him if the weather was right it was a good life. So it was off to South Wales, Tenby to be precise, somebody was smiling on us, we had a lovely sunny fortnight camped on a cliff top with views of the bay and a sandy beach. If I wasn't swimming and sun bathing I was trailing around the many castles and castle ruins that were in the area.

It seemed like no time at all when the holiday was over and we were making our way home. It was just a little bit too fast according to one Police Sergeant he gave father a right telling off for speeding! Karen and I were both surprised that father, in mitigation, didn't tell the Sergeant that the speedometer on the car wasn't working.

More good news when we returned home, the house was ready for us to move into so that's what we did, no more revolting caravan. Karen insisted that I had the bedroom next to the noisy main road, that way she could have the quieter bedroom, overlooking the drive and the orchard, and sleep in peace. It was me who was kept awake at night watching headlights chase each other around my room, not to mention the noise. That same year Karen had caught measles, as mother was only going to go through this once she ordered me into the other end of the bed so I caught it as well.

The most farcical part of that year was when father wanted me to join a Cub group, I didn't want to but I got fed up with hearing that I would never make anything of myself. I decided to give it a try, father did promise he would come and collect me, as I would have missed the last bus by the time Cubs ended. I must admit I was enjoying Cubs, although it would be another year before I could go to camp as I had missed that year's.

What I didn't like was walking home at night along the busy main road with lorries passing within a whisker of me, and father was never on time.

I would always be home first so mother always assumed I had been collected safely. Whichever season it was, the walk home was always creepy. The broad leaves of summer darkened the wooded parts of the road, and in winter the leafless branches were equally creepy—like gnarled fingers pointing into the moonlit sky. This sight always ensured I didn't loiter. Drivers would stop their cars to offer me a lift, but being only eight years old I had to refuse.

Was I hearing things that night? I thought I could hear the faint sound of a violin, it seemed to be following me home, the night air was cold but I felt a warm rush of air around me as I was thrown into a nearby ditch, just as a car came screeching to a halt. The driver was frantic with worry; he scrambled down into the ditch blubbering through tears.

"I am so sorry, I was forced off the road, I didn't see you until it was too late, speak to me, please tell me you're not dead," he said as he landed on top of me. I don't think he was forced off the road at all; he was more likely a drunk driver, as what he sicked all over me smelled mainly of rum.

"I'm not dead so could you get off me?" I replied. He looked like he had seen a ghost.

"But you couldn't have seen me, you had your back to me, I must have hit you." "Well you didn't and I'm alright except for a few scratches."

I helped him out of the ditch and brushed him down, he offered to give me a lift home, which surprised me as I was covered in his vomit, for obvious reasons I declined, so he drove off. I was smelly, cold, wet and terrified, I didn't like the sound of the violin, I didn't like the drunk driver and I was alone by the side of the road in pitch darkness. I ran as I have never run before. I was motivated by pure fear and adrenalin.

As I reached the school premises I continued running through the grounds, home territory, I hoped I could trust. I discarded my coat as I passed some bushes; it would need to be washed in the swimming pool, but not tonight, maybe tomorrow after school.

As I raced across the kitchen garden and orchard my chest began to burn as I took in more of the cold night air. I thought as I ran, if someone is going to catch me I would make it as difficult as possible for them.

Once at the side gate to our house I fell against the kitchen wall my heart was pounding and I felt sure it would burst out of me there and then. As I stood there I thought that maybe this is what my grandfather meant about a guardian angel, but I could not take his advice about not to be frightened.

I was told off by mother for leaving my coat at cubs, I was still covered in muddy water, through 'larking around'. I let her believe that, as the truth would have kept us up all night.

The whole saga of Cubs ended when I got home one night, not knowing that father had only just left to collect me, mother told me off for arranging a lift home and not telling anyone. It was then I told her I had walked home, father had never collected me, I had always walked home. Poor mother she stood there with her mouth open, father had some explaining to do, me, well I never went to Cubs again.

Father had the last laugh though. At weekends he would go night fishing down on the coast and one of my chores was to switch off the swimming pool pump. I was not to switch it off until after half past nine, not so great, as it was dark and spooky by then. I have got a terrible imagination, I could scare myself in an empty room and as I would approach the pump which was situated near the wooded area by the pool, I would hear the noise it was making long before I reached it. The pump was in a wooden casing shaped like the roof of a house and I would have to lift up one side of the 'roof' with one hand and turn off the pump with the other. Before I got there I would say to myself, the moment I press that button and all becomes quiet anyone hiding in the bushes is going to know exactly where I am.

The ordeal that evening from cubs had not cured my phobia of the dark. That was it I don't believe Stirling Moss in his racing car would not have beaten me home and to make matters worse I would appear in the sitting room trying to get my breath, to find Karen watching the telly. She saw I was out of breath, and twigged I had been running:

"Have you switched off the pool pump like father asked you to?"

"Yes."

"So you've run all the way home. YOU'RE SCARED OF THE DARK!" Ah my little baby brudder is scared of the dark." There are sometimes when you can do without sisters and this was one of them.

It was plain to see that Farthings had once been a private house with lots of staff. Some of the classrooms had been converted from stables and I could tell this straight away, as I used to live above empty stables. There was a gym that had a stage at one end on which the girls would act out plays near Christmas, and the gym was filled with seats for those parents who were able to attend.

Opposite the huts that we saw on the way in were sports fields, grass tennis courts and then the big one a boy's paradise! A large wood and a lake within it, stocked with at least Carp and Rudd, well they were the only fish I caught there. I had arrived!

As I was making my way around the lake, looking for any fishing tackle that might have been caught up in the branches of overhanging trees, I saw a wooden hut, most of which was in the water.

On closer inspection, to my delight I saw it was a boat house and inside was a white painted wooden clinker—built boat, together with a pair of varnished oars. I told father of my find and he promptly banned me from going anywhere near it.

We always knew when the girls were returning; cars would be up and down the drive all evening and father would come home worn out after heaving heavy trunks. Although I had not met any of the girls it was comforting to have them at the school, there was obviously more buzz with them around and the place wasn't all quiet and spooky. I did though appreciate the headmistress keeping the swimming pool open for us to enjoy during the holidays as on the way there we could pick a ripe Victoria plum or an apple in the orchard and then swimming in the pool or getting a suntan with the transistor radio blaring. To keep in shape there was always a game of tennis, or a spot of fishing if you needed some peace; what a place.

Who wanted to go visiting when you were surrounded by all this grandeur, especially my grandparents on my father's side? Although they were fine I just didn't like Portsmouth. It seemed a lonely old place with single women pushing prams whilst their husbands were away at sea. My grandparents lived on a rambling council estate and an auntie and uncle lived at another nearby. This was where I was beaten up for wearing odd socks, would you believe? I cannot really say I yearned to visit these places instead of staying at home enjoying my palatial surroundings.

CHAPTER 2

In 1962 mother's pregnancy was showing. The girls at my primary school all had good ideas on how the baby would be born. Out through the tummy was understandable, but my imagination couldn't stretch to mother giving birth through her breasts! All the same, in June, Abigail (Abi) was born at the cottage hospital in the nearby town. Karen and I were not allowed into the maternity unit, mother had a bed by a window so we could talk to her from outside.

The following summer Karen and I were horrified to come home from school one day to see little Abi with an arm in plaster. Mother had left her for as long as it took to answer the door to tell the visitor to wait and in that time Abi had rolled off the sofa, landing badly and breaking an arm.

We had brought with us, from our previous home, Karen's cat Blackie and father's dog, a black cocker spaniel called Smoky. He had a white diamond on his forehead and although we only got him a few months ago he was father's dog, and used to go to work with father at the old place. I thought now would be a good opportunity to take him for walks, and hopefully make him my pet.

Although we lived next to a busy main road this didn't appear to be a problem, as there was the orchard and fields Smoky could run around in. In the field next to the swimming pool and at its furthest end, was a brick wall on a mound. Father said Polish troops used it for target practice whilst being billeted at the school during the war.

I went there to see if there were any bullets or cartridge cases lying around, giving Smoky a walk at the same time but I had no luck in finding any ammunition, so we made our way home. I had ignored the cows on the way over and they ignored me, but they were now taking an interest in me, they formed a herd and started following us. As I ran, they followed at a faster speed. I had never experienced anything like this before; I began to panic, as although I could see our saviour—the fence—in sight, I wasn't sure we would reach it in time. I ran for all I was worth and Smoky kept along side of me.

The fence took some getting over as it had a strong wire mesh up to four feet high, not the ordinary barb wire that I could have quickly rolled under. I was struggling to climb it, with the cows almost on top of me, I don't know what they would have done to me and I didn't want to find out and then my little hero came to the rescue, barking like mad and darting in all directions to keep the cows at bay was Smoky. I loved him to bits, as far as I was concerned he saved my life, he wasn't father's dog anymore, he was mine, I let him lick my face all over, we were inseparable.

A weekend trip to the coast always went down the same route. My mother sometimes threatened to put me in a 'home' if I misbehaved, an idle threat I'm sure, until our trips to the coast went past a boy's prison. A borstal.

"That's where you'll go one day," she said, indicating this place. I was absolutely horrified and realised she probably meant what she said after all, it was a huge overbearing ugly looking place. I would stay awake at night watching the stairs for men to come and take me away. I learned that mother was often put in a home as a child when her mother couldn't cope with a job, a daughter and a war hero. Once I knew this I was able to forgive her for the terror she put me through. I couldn't bear to think of no Karen, no Abi, no surroundings like the girls' school and no parents.

Boxing Day 1962 saw the start of a glorious white winter—well it was for a boy. After a week, and once the snow began to take effect my school was closed. As our heating system was coal-fired the lorries couldn't get through and we were sent home until further notice.

That didn't mean I had nothing to do. I would help keep the drive and walkways clear and at the lake there were ice skaters who, although trespassing, were skating on the frozen lake. They were very skilled and a joy to watch, it was obvious they were there for that purpose only and when they finished they left the property with no harm done. Therefore I didn't see the need to tell anyone.

It did get me thinking though, if they could do it think of the fun I could have messing about on the ice? I watched where they had got off so I knew where a good strong piece of ice was for getting onto the lake, however I got about twelve yards out, crashed through the ice, and as I tried to pull myself out it gave away and further kept breaking up, till I reached the bank, soaked and freezing. I knew my parents would go mad when I got home. They didn't disappoint.

In the November of 1963, John Kennedy the American President was assassinated. I was ten years old I didn't like death. The school was for the living and gave me so much freedom; far more that anyone else had living on a council estate of my age.

I was disgusted to hear that one of the builders who was doing some work at the school had brought his son Colin with him. My father and his both heard Colin say, "Not still talking about bloody Kennedy are you?" That earned him a mouth wash with soap and water. Not only for that, he was within earshot of the girls, how much more trouble did he want to be in for one day?

That said, when I eventually met some of the girls, quite often I would hear them using swear words, which would always be followed by, "Sorry George". It always brought a smile to my face, to know that I had caught them out.

Still, in that November, I heard mother and father arguing that Smoky must be kept an eye on, as there was a bitch in season in a nearby lane. I didn't know what that meant. It was a Saturday evening when there was a knock at the front door. I heard parts of the conversation this man was having with my father and I got closer to listen some more but mother told me to go away. The man went on, "I didn't see him, he is a black dog would you know who owns him?"

A moment later father appeared, Smoky had been involved in an accident and he was going to take him to the vets. I went cold and my heart sank. Two hours later father appeared in the doorway to the sitting room, I cried like mad before he got the words out, his face said it all, my hero and my life saver was dead, intact except for a small single hole in the white diamond on his forehead. Smoky had been on the main road, something he never did, but it was possible he had been to see the bitch my parents had talked about. I let the world know that night that I was totally upset.

A short while after that Blackie, Karen's cat, perished on that road. From now on pets were to be bunnies or hamsters, no cats or dogs.

The following year father asked me to take the builder's son Colin, to camp. He was about my age and was getting in with the wrong sort of people, hence the swearing episode. We got on really well and spent a lot of weekends camping and fishing at the lake. The woods surrounding the lake were very spooky at night, not the sort of place you would want to visit if you didn't have to and it wasn't just the woods, you also had to consider the school and who may be prowling around for that reason. Colin didn't help by saying every so often. "What was that? I thought I heard something."

Whilst being in one of these states of high alert, the sandstone rock I used for sitting on round the fire suddenly split underneath me due to the heat. It went off with a bang and startled me, giving Colin the impression I had been shot by someone. I really don't think he slept well that night.

Father and my uncle took us both sea fishing. My uncle had a small, clinker-built fishing boat, open except for a small cabin at the bows. We were going to stay out all night.

We had dropped anchor somewhere in the Solent, the sea was very choppy, the boat was being tossed side to side, backwards and forwards, held only by a piece of chain. My stomach tolerated this for a short while then I was ill and couldn't stop being ill. I was told we couldn't go back as there would be no water at the mooring and after several hours of this if I could have jumped overboard and drowned, it would have been a welcome release. This was my introduction to the sea, and I hated every minute of it.

When I returned home I went to the lake to gather my thoughts, something I did quite often. It was on one such occasion when a man came up to me, he was about 25 years old and we spent a lot of time chatting. He used to live at the school and missed it badly, not just for the girls, as he use to turn up when they were on their holidays, but the whole atmosphere of the place, just the things that I was enjoying, like the swimming pool, the lake, woods, and the tennis courts. He gave me a potted history of the place—apparently the house had not long been converted into a school—it was previously owned by an elderly couple who had moved up from Portsmouth. When they died they left a substantial amount of money and a will saying it had to be turned into a private girls' school. The man's family had worked for the previous owners and stayed on when it became a school, they were now retired hence me and my family were here.

Of course he was now an outsider. Times had moved on, nobody knew him, although he had once roamed free here and knew everyone, he was now trespassing on private property, and I should report him. I put this to him as tactfully as I could. He gave me his word he would not come back, I believed him, and I never saw him again. I didn't give it much thought at the time, but was I going to be that man one day? When it was my turn to leave I would cut the place out of my life, or so I thought, I was just so unaware that this place had more in store for me than I could ever imagine.

CHAPTER 3

Christmas 1963 was fast approaching; with it was the school play. Mother pleaded with Karen and I to go and see it. I knew I would feel awkward as lots of posh people would be there. When the time came, mother virtually frog—marched us to the gym. There she left us to fend for ourselves. We walked past all the posh cars that were all here in abundance.

Inside, the place was all hustle and bustle with parents taking a single-minded interest in what their daughters had been up to for their money. Fathers seemed at ease wearing a suit, whilst the mothers were wearing furs and lots of jewellery. Their expensive perfumes filled the air.

This was a night for girls and their parents. I honestly thought I was going to be asked to leave, and although I never was, I still felt awkward and out of place.

Karen would be alright being a girl, but there were no brothers that would somehow justify me being there, only parents. I really did think to myself I don't want to be here. At last everyone was filing into the gym and into their seats. Good, I thought, it will be dark in there and no one will notice me. Mother had told us we couldn't take any of the seats, the only way we could see the play was to hang on the wall bars at the back.

This year was to be a story of a young woman, Catherine Tobias, who came into an inheritance, and although she was being pursued by an eligible young Mr Morris Howard, it was unsure if he wanted her affections or her money! She decided on the latter, and when they were due to elope she decided against it.

I had never seen a play of any sort before. Karen and I were mesmerised by the quality of acting, especially the girls who played the male parts, so much so we didn't know that when the cast went quiet it was to mean the end of act one. Had we been aware we could have climbed down from the wall bars, instead the lights came on in the gym and we were hung there like a couple of traitors from a medieval scene. Once one set of parents looked round it seemed like they all did. Oh how I wanted the ground to open up and swallow me! I really had it with the school. I never wanted to come up here again.

The following spring whilst I was looking for father, out near some flower boarders, I literally bumped into the girl who had played the leading part in the play. Her name was Joan Edenbridge. This was my first encounter with any of the girls, the first time I really saw one of them in the flesh, and it looked like I was about to have my first conversation with a highly educated girl that was going to leave me all embarrassed and awkward. I really had nothing to say to her, nothing she wanted to hear anyway, she was just going to have a bit of toffee-nosed fun at my expense.

She was pretty and looking straight at me. I thought she was just going to say hello and walk away.

Instead she said. "Your Tom's son George, aren't you?"

"Yes," I said. I thought, oh no what's coming, what is she going to say to me? Don't you dare ever hijack one of my plays again, came to mind.

"My name is Joan, pleased to meet you." I think at this stage my mouth just fell open, I was looking for the long socks, the straw boater, the snobby attitude, where were they? The vindictive kids from the council estate were the snobs, but they had nothing to be snobby about, Joan shouldn't have given me a second look but here she was going out of her way to be friends, I was so confused:

"Aren't you going to talk?"

"Yes, I saw you in the play, you were very good."

"Thank you, young sir did you enjoy it?"
"Yes I did."

She continued: "We have to be on our toes, as the drama teacher we've got worked in theatres in the West End and does not accept second best," I could certainly believe that.

"Well, come by the classrooms and say hello, I'll introduce you to my friends, will you do that for me?"

"Yes, yes I will."

"Right I will hold you to that, come and say hello, we don't bite," she said as she walked away.

Joan had just made me feel like I was the only person who mattered in her life, what a lovely person. I felt really stupid now for having pre-conceived ideas, but I wasn't going to give up, I consoled myself with the thought, I bet they're not all like that.

I was studying hard for the eleven plus and training for sports day, when it all came to nothing, I was knocked from my bike coming home from school.

The accident happened at a busy crossroads, four broken ribs went through my lungs, and influenza was filling them up. I was knocked unconscious but there was a doctor and a nurse not far away, I was told their initial action and that of a young girl helped save my life. The little girl had put me in the recovery position. I was told later that had she not done this no one could have done anything for me, as I would have choked to death on my own bile, blood and vomit.

I was taken to the cottage hospital where Abi was born, and later transferred to a larger hospital, which was better equipped to treat my type of injuries; I was given 24 hours to live.

The doctors melodramatically told my parents: "We've done our bit; it's up to him if he wants to live or not." My father told me they were the exact words and my mother fainted.

In those twenty-four hours I could sense that someone was helping me fight for my life, although unconscious I knew I was not alone. For the second time in my life I heard the sound of a violin playing—what world have I been placed in? I saw a light, and at the end of the light was a group of angels facing me, beckoning me to come to heaven. Then I would see another light, some sort of vision turning the angels round with their backs to me, which meant that they did not want to take me. I wasn't dead yet, but every so often the angels would reappear wanting me to join them. Again the vision would turn them around. This seemed to go on for an eternity until I woke up.

The vision had got her way. I was alive.

Apart from the joy of seeing my family when they came to visit, mother brought in a hand-written card from Joan. It's the thought from others that can sometimes make all the difference. Joan's card gave me a lift knowing that whilst I was stuck in hospital someone as sweet as her was thinking of me, again what a lovely person.

The whole of my class wrote a letter each for me. Some wanted to, some had to, it didn't matter, I enjoyed reading them all the same.

The woman who hit me was going to pick up her daughter from Farthings school. I never met her, but I do feel sorry for her, any accident involving a child is traumatic to say the least.

The school summer holidays had started by the time I left hospital, I was therefore unable to thank the kids for their letters. This had been Joan's last year at the school so I was unable to keep my promise to call by the classrooms. I traced the doctor and the nurse to say thank-you, but I could not find the young girl. I quizzed my friends who had seen the accident to see if she was a girl from our school, but they had never seen her either.

I wasn't out of the woods yet. Another chest infection would have dire consequences, so no swimming, or camping, just rest.

A few weeks after leaving hospital two policemen called on me to find out if I could remember anything about the accident. I told them I couldn't even remember what happened that day. It seems that is usual if the body is badly traumatised, the memory wipes out the whole incident, what a fantastic piece of work the human body is.

I was really pleased I could do nothing all through the really hot sunny weeks of the school holiday but be fit to start at the secondary modern in the main town when school re-opened. Some kind soul had assessed me as a result of missing the eleven plus. (My father often referred to my accident as a clever dodge to miss exams, I called it fighting for my life.) I was put in a class I didn't think I should have been placed in. I soon proved I was right by moving up a class when I eventually did take some exams.

One evening at home Abi would not stop crying, she was sweating quite a lot. "You will have to go and get mother, I don't know what to do with her," Karen told me.

This was going to be my first visit to the school, where I would actually face a lot of girls as they congregated in the classrooms of an evening. I checked the classrooms off the court yard—they were mainly empty. That left the huts.

"Fells, now is not a good time to bend over your desk and show your knickers, George is here."

This was followed by a raucous laughter from the other girls in the room. These well chosen words came from a rather tall girl with dark frizzy hair, at full volume, about two inches from my face. Having an older sister the mention of some poor girl's knicker elastic didn't have the desired effect of embarrassing me one little bit. "Hello George we've heard all about you, what can we do for you? Are you looking for your mother, she's in the end hut." I think I got out the words "thank you" as I left.

Mother greeted me with "Hello love, what brings you up here?"

"Abi won't stop crying and she's sweating, Karen doesn't know what to do, she wants you to come home."

"Karen will have to look after her until I've finished sweeping these huts."

"I can do that for you if you want to go home. By the way do you know a girl called Fells?"

"Yes that would be Felicity, she's a lovely girl she has a long pony tail all the way down her back, why have you got your eye on her?"

"'I think Abi is still crying mother."

I entered a hut, empty except for one girl. She was at her desk reading a book, pretty girl with a long pony tail all the way down her back. I thought I would be as quiet as possible and try not to disturb her, when she said, "Hello, you've changed, the last time I saw you, you were a female."

"Hi, my name's George, mothers had to go home so I'm finishing off for her."

"Oh, she's your mother, sorry, my name's Felicity." "Pleased to meet you," I said.

I carried on sweeping when she appeared by my side. "I'm leaving now, but I just wanted you to know it's not on account that you're in the room, I have some prep I need to go and finish, so I will say goodnight."

"Um yes goodnight." I noticed when she left she was wearing the winter uniform, which was a close fitted skirt that finished below her knee, I couldn't help thinking if she had done cartwheels in that skirt all night she would still have kept her modesty intact.

I took it as a bit of a complement that the girls wanted a laugh and were prepared to include me. I had to have a re-think of what I thought about them. They had impeccable manners, showing me so much respect. I really did think they would look on me as a male intruder, breaking in on their female domain, but they went out of their way to show me it wasn't a problem. It was as if they were reading my mind about girls and trying to put me at ease.

I started to get on really well with all the girls I met, even the one who set me up. She was fine, just a bit loud but a heart of gold that was Elaine. It was about 9 o'clock when I finished all the sweeping and I made my way out of the school along a poorly lit corridor where the girls' stinky games boots were stored. On the other side of the corridor was the gym and now I was at the top end of the drive.

Like my walks home from the Cubs it made no difference what the season was, the full leaf branches of the horse chestnut trees made the drive dark in summer and when the trees were bare in winter, they were equally as spooky because of the moon shining between the empty branches. On this occasion the leaves were still on the trees making the drive very dark. If only I had not said to myself, 'I bet someone's waiting behind one of those trees to grab me', I could have had a quiet walk home, instead I had to endure the exhausting run home, scaring myself witless over nothing. I got indoors; mother greeted me with, "Hello love, would you like a cup of tea?"

I struggled to get out the words, "Yes please." I was so out of breath.

Mother said: "You sound exhausted, have you been running?"

"Don't you start?" I replied. She gave me a quizzical look and handed me my tea. "What was wrong with Abi?" I asked.

"Nothing that a mother's cuddle couldn't sort out," she replied.

I began to visit the school quite a lot in the evenings. Mother said, "If you will come up here you can find a broom and help me out." So I did.

The girls had made me feel comfortable in their presence right from the start; I therefore developed a loyalty towards them. I took exception to the crude remarks and the taunting I received at my own school; friends were still heavily vetted. I was very much influenced music wise by the girls; it would be British rock and roll blaring out from one classroom then the classics from another, followed by American soul music. What a life.

Father was soon dragging me up to the airport to pick up girls flying in, mostly from Europe. He would have felt uncomfortable travelling back to the school with some little tot, so he had brought me along to break the ice. I was surprised to see us picking up one young girl, she had flown in from Germany, she could only have been aged eleven and had travelled alone. I suppose if she was put on the plane at one airport and met the other end, there wasn't much that could go wrong in between. Her name was Jill, we were soon chatting, and in no time we had reached the school. Had it been just her and father it could have been a silent, awkward ride for both of them.

I always enjoyed speaking to the girls getting to know their way of life, who they were and where they had come from. Curiosity killed the cat, in my case there was no more a truer saying than the day I caught sight of a little stunner with a page boy hair style, her name was Jennifer Bradley. She went about her schooldays disappearing to write her own poems. She distanced herself from the boisterous girls, and because of her beautiful innocence she quickly became the darling of the school. I was smitten; I just had to get to know her.

As with all new entrants Jennifer started her school life in the 'huts' opposite the sports fields and it didn't take me long to notice the hut she was in. I would sit outside and wait for her dinner break. We would sit and talk and she would nuzzle her face into my neck, sometimes she would put her hands on my face pulling me towards her, giving me an opened mouth kiss with those soft tender lips. I'm glad she had the strength for both of us because I didn't want to let her go back to her classroom. I would remain sitting on the grass and pass her notes through the window where she sat. On one note I asked her to marry me, how sweet at the age of twelve.

I had to realise that Jennifer was delicate and gentle for when I played football I was often given a hug from my mates for scoring a goal. It was a manly hug that took my breath away and the contact was always hot and sweaty after a lot of running, but I had to adapt, I had to be gentle in return. I now had soft warm, hands caressing my face, gentle soft lips were kissing me, and two firm lumps were poking into my chest, the owner taking them for granted, but this was all new to me. I looked at her. I saw her make-up applied with care, her eye shadow picked to match the colour of her hair, the smell of perfumed girlie soap, instead of the common or garden soap smell from a football changing room.

The sleeves of her cardigan were pushed up to the elbow in an industrious ready-for-work sort of way, ready to work on me, so this was the tender trap. I saw her eyes close as she anticipated a kiss, her breathing became short and heavy, I saw her willingness to stand on tip toe to be held and kissed. I thought I knew what girls were all about having two sisters, but nothing prepared me for this, to exchange love and intimacy willingly.

I checked on the other girls, my friends, enquiring if make-up was allowed in school, it wasn't. All the rebellious care Jennifer took in her looks appeared to be for my benefit. When our lips met it was like being drawn into her world of love and tenderness, it would have come as no surprise to me if I had opened my eyes and saw that we had floated away on an emotion of gentle soft passion. My head was in a spin, and I was receiving all the love and charm from this little stunner.

I was in shock as nothing like this had happened to me before, none of the other girls showed any sign of wanting a relationship like this, in fact I regarded them as chums. They were friends somebody to talk to, where both sides could gauge their ability to talk to the opposite sex, in a friendly no pressure environment, but now there was just the two of us. There was no friendly female to help me out if I got flustered, I was in the company of a beautiful girl who hung on my every word, I found the situation very unnerving, whereas Jennifer seemed to be very much at ease, taking it all in her stride.

CHAPTER 4

Finding Jennifer was care free, the days were full of light hearted-innocence, but then disaster struck. I was getting feelings that I had never known before, I didn't like these feelings; they were stopping me from being the person I was, what on earth was happening to me? Jennifer wasn't like the rest of the girls. I could talk to them and carry on with my life, they were my friends and had no effect on me, but Jennifer wasn't a friend. I couldn't meet her with the same casual approach like I could with the other girls; she had a different effect on me.

It wasn't long before I couldn't cope with her. I developed a tight knot in my stomach that wouldn't go away, I was 'off ' my food, I didn't want to leave the school. I didn't really want to do anything; all my interests had gone. Fishing, football, seeing my friends—nothing mattered anymore, unless there was the slightest excuse for me to visit the school and then I was off like a shot. If I saw Jennifer it made everything alright, if I didn't I was down in the dumps again. Mother saw the signs that being lovesick brings and despite my various excuses that it was nothing of the sort, all I could do was think of Jennifer.

All these emotions and pains I was putting myself through were a complete and utter waste of time as I knew this little lady was being financed and groomed for a far better life than the one I was used to, but I didn't care. I was in love with her; there wasn't anything I could do about it.

I missed her during school holidays, which now seemed to be a complete waste of time, what a contrast. I now looked forward to term time and Jennifer was the first person I looked for when the girls returned. Whenever I saw her she always looked gorgeous, as for those eyes, she was with a group of friends near the entrance to the courtyard when she looked in my direction she fixed me a look with those big brown eyes. I was captivated by the smouldering look she was giving me.

She wasn't breaking my heart; a broken heart can be mended. No little miss gorgeous was giving me that look, whilst she reached into me and removed my heart and smashed it into a million pieces. She then hid every piece so that it could not be repaired, and at the same time the look on her innocent little face seemed to be saying,

"Who me?"

As if I wasn't suffering enough! When I walked into a classroom and Jennifer was there my heart pounded so much I thought it would burst out of me. I would talk to her, but not too much as I didn't want to expose the nervous wreck I was in her presence. When I left the classroom I even checked on the conversation I had with her to make sure I had not said anything that would have sounded idiotic.

I was coping alright with the girls, just a few twangs of the heart strings, nothing I couldn't cope with when boy meets girl, so why did this little stunner have to walk into my life and turn everything on its head? Why couldn't she have gone to another school and given some other boy the pains of being in love with her? Why couldn't someone have told me she was at this school? Would I have heeded the warning I don't know, but it must be some bodies' fault why I was in this emotional mess!

Jennifer was intelligent, stunningly beautiful and witty, everything a boy needed to make him feel totally insecure and inadequate, and this was what she was like as a young girl.

No school uniform for me or Karen, what we stood up in is what we went to school in, father was far too selfish. He had ordered a mahogany clinker-built fishing boat specially made in the Orkneys, on completion to be shipped all the way to Sussex and I'm sure it was a lot more expensive than father would have us believe. He always maintained he gave up smoking cigarettes to afford the boat, but in the absence of cigarettes in the house, I found it hard to believe him. It was his toy and we had to go without so he could afford it, why not compromise and buy a second-hand boat?

The headmaster at my school was a kind man, but he also had a no-nonsense approach to running the school. He gave out lots of chances but if you persistently defied him over truancy, long hair, etc., you were expelled. However, over school uniform he was always prepared to listen to cases of hardship. I liked him even though he would humiliate me by pulling me out of line in assembly. He would point to the other boys, my friends, and say, "Why are you wearing jeans to this school? Do you see the other boys dressed like you? I need to speak to your father, do you have a father?"

"Yes sir."

"Good I want him here to discuss this matter."

I told all this to father time and again to which he would always refuse to attend the school. Father would always say: "You tell your headmaster, with all dues and respects sir, I wear what my father can afford; you tell him that from me."

He said with his usual aggressive manner, as a twelve year old, he expected me to come out with a comment like that!

The Headmistress who employed father saw our plight and one term she bought Karen and me a complete uniform. Knowing the lovely old lady as I did, I bet it came out of her own pocket. However the old skinflint still didn't take the hint and by the next term we were back in our rags, the humiliation went on. I had to do something about it as I was going round with my friends and visiting their houses after school and I would always notice their mothers giving me the once over.

I learnt that 13 year-olds could have a paper round. I cycled to the village the girls would walk to for church on a Sunday morning. I told the newsagent that I needed the largest round he had got and, by chance, a boy was just giving up one such round, he was leaving school. I went with him for a couple of days to learn the route, then it was all mine. I cycled a total of eight miles every morning as my deliveries took me out to all the farms. I left home at six and I had to be home by eight o'clock in time for breakfast and the bus to school. In no time I had clothes that were a good match for the original school uniform.

The headmaster was pleased to see the change in me. "Your father took heed of my letters then?" He said.
"Yes Sir," I lied.

"Good, I'm glad he did, I didn't want to lose you." 'WHAT' I thought, letters lose me? I didn't realise just how close I had come to losing my friends and going to this brilliant school.

I was getting use to the early mornings, and soon found I could have a bit of fun delivering newspapers. Billings Farm was a large house that had a highly polished hallway with a letter box that was so small I had to separate the papers, especially on a Friday when I had several papers and magazines to deliver. I used to balance each paper on the edge of the letter box, if I hit the ends hard enough they would skate off the hallway into the kitchen.

I followed United throughout their campaign in Europe, when they played mid-week I just had to read every report on them. I had to deliver a girlie magazine to another address so that got well thumbed before I put it through his door, and I couldn't help but laugh at Grayson's Farm for I put their paper through the door only to hear puppy growls and the ripping of paper.

Up at Mallets, which was an old people's home, an elderly woman greeted me one morning with. "Go away; we don't want your sort here if you're going to wear women's clothes."

It wasn't long before the boss spoke to me.

"Billings Farm, can we try and get the papers on his doormat? He doesn't like picking them out of the dog's water bowl in the kitchen, let's keep him sweet. The boy who does your round at the week-end, he doesn't like taking the flak from customers he collects from for your weekly antics. Sorry about the old lady I forgot to tell you about her, you don't wear women's clothes do you?"

"What," I said

"O.k. o.k. you're a bit too young for my sense of humour, do you like the new trades bike I bought for your round?"

"Yes," I lied.

"Then why do you still use your own?"

"To be honest the new bike is too heavy."

"Yes, I see, of course when I rode it, it seemed o.k. But then I am twenty stone, what are you seven? If you keep using that bike you're going to disappear altogether, put some weight on for goodness sake. Do you mind if I give that bike to someone else?"

"No that's fine by me."

"Right, you're doing all the hard graft on your round, you've saved me the cost of a bike, so I'm going to give you an extra ten shillings a week, are you happy with that?"

"Yes I'm more than happy."

"Right, I needed to talk to you just to let you know whose side I'm on," he said winking at me. "Now get yourself off home, it's far too late for you to do your round, I'll do it for you and you won't lose the money."

That also happened if the 'paper' train was late in the mornings, I would always be sent home but I wouldn't lose any money.

Slater's farm had a golden Labrador called Honey. She always waited for me, and I would put the paper in her mouth so she could take it to the farm. One morning I hadn't reached her, she was coming to greet me, but on this occasion she decided to sink her teeth into my right leg.

When father went to see Mr Slater that evening he threatened him with having Honey put down, but I said I didn't want that to happen and what didn't help father's cause was I was stroking

Honey as she was licking my face. My boss said he would tell Slater to collect his paper from the shop if he couldn't keep his dog under control, but I told him it wasn't a problem; I would be a bit more wary of her in future.

CHAPTER 5

I loved the preparation for the school plays. I would pay quite a few visits to the stage, although I had nothing to do there except take in the atmosphere of the carpenters building the scenery and making intricate motors for specialist parts, such as a reclining chair for a play involving a gruesome barber. Cook would send along some sandwiches which were made from thick white bread, with an even thicker layer of butter that your teeth sank right into, before you got to the filling, which was nearly always chicken.

Father collected me from school once, so he did know his way there after all. He had to collect a piece of scenery from a contact known by the drama teacher from her 'West End' days and he felt it wise to take me with him. We were well into our journey when I thought I would ask where we were going. "Highbury", said father. "Near the football ground, I thought that as you have been there to watch United play you would know the way."

That man lived in a world of his own. "I travel to matches by train and underground," I said. "I don't know the way." We spent hours going around in circles (to make matters worse it started to snow heavily) until we reached the place late into the evening where we were met by a man that would not have looked out of place in Dickensian times. He wore a grubby old overcoat tied in the middle by a piece of string. He was a tall fat man with a bald head and a long bent nose and I began to look round for some street urchins.

The place was some kind of warehouse, dimly lit with straw used to protect ornaments scattered everywhere. The man handed father a witch's cauldron, I waited to see what else we needed but that was it, we had come all this way for a witch's cauldron, what a waste of time, when I'm sure there was one in Karen's bedroom.

It was half past nine when we arrived at the school, the drama teacher insisted on seeing the cauldron that night and whilst father did that I went to see if there were any girls I could talk to. As I was making my way across the courtyard my blood ran cold, I looked around for imminent danger as I could hear a violin being played. I was relieved to hear the sound coming from the music room, but it was the same tune I heard that night walking home from Cubs, and whilst I was fighting for my life in hospital. I was trembling as I walked towards the door, the girl who was playing had her back to me but as I walked in she turned around; it was Jennifer's closest friend Amanda.

She smiled but gave me a concerned look, mainly because I was studying her very closely:

"Can I help you?" She said.

"I am sorry, I didn't mean to stare, have you been playing the violin very long?" "Why does it sound like a cat screaming? Yes, I have been practising for some years now."

"Can I have a go?" I asked.

"No, my dear, this is a very expensive instrument, the only one in the country and I love it because it has a unique sound all of its own. Now you didn't want to come in here and talk about violins did you?"

Amanda was turning out to be a real friend; she could also read me like a book. "She's not here, and if I knew where she was I would tell you, but you can stay and talk to me if you like."

"You're really in love with her aren't you George?" I nodded in agreement and said: "What do you know about her?"

"Well that's just it," said Amanda. "None of us can really claim to know her. She tends to keep herself to herself. I'll find out what I can but I warn you she is very much a closed book."

"Thanks," I said.

Mother wasn't blind either. "I hope you're only talking 'shop' to these girls," she would say. "And Jennifer, they may be polite and sweet to you, but don't get the wrong idea, that's part of their breeding. When they go home they have their own lives to lead, don't go thinking you are on the same level as they are, because you are not." When she started off like that I would think to myself, I have already worked that one out mother but thanks for trying to keep my feet on the ground.

Whenever I saw a group of girls I would always quickly cast an eye over them to see if Jennifer was amongst them, even on the games fields, but I had to stop doing that as one girl playing Lacrosse unintentionally flashed me her bottle green knickers. The girls were there for their games, I didn't want to make them conscious that I was there, in my part looking for Jennifer, but with them thinking that I was being less than a gentleman. Besides I may be reported, and that would put a stop to my school visits.

I never saw Jennifer on the sports field, I suppose after what I did see, it was just as well, for supposing that poor girl had been Jennifer, goodness me what state my sanity would have been in?

Now whenever I walked into a classroom my friends would all shout "She's not here!" Or some sweet soul would know where she was and offer to go and get her for me—they always came back empty handed. She was either not to be found, or the embarrassment factor would have proved too much. Then I would visit a quiet classroom far away from the noise and the gossip of our mutual friends, and there I would find her, quietly giving me one of her best smouldering looks as I walked in. Now I was convinced she knew she was turning me to jelly and enjoying every minute of it. This lovely lass was becoming aware of her womanly powers, and I was in the line of fire. If I could have looked into the future and seen all this coming would I have changed any of it? Not for a minute.

The first winter after meeting Jennifer she sent me a Christmas card, inside she had drawn a matchstick man with a halo above his head, with the word 'you' next to him, that got pride of place in my bedroom.

The next time I saw Jennifer was in her classroom. She was on her own; we seemed to be able to read each other's mind as she left her seat. She came up to me and gave me a peck on the cheek, but it didn't stop there, although I could hardly rip off her uniform. I let her soft lips work their way round my mouth and at last her sweet searching tongue found mine.

We could hear some of her friends approaching the classroom. Luckily I had my excuse—the broom, and Jennifer had her books.

I had to smile at her, we had just been passionate but she made sure she covered her knees with her skirt as the girls walked past the classroom. I wanted 'seconds' but Jennifer insisted it would be too risky. "Don't be greedy George, there's always tomorrow," she said.

I could afford to be rational because I was only twelve, had I been older I doubt very much that I could have kept my hands to myself. Amanda was right, Jennifer was a very private lass, other girls would leave their schoolwork open at their desks, but I could never find anything with Jennifer's name on. As she seemed to be a quiet girl it would have been a good way of reading her work and finding out something about how her mind worked. I asked her for a photograph of herself, I was given a one word answer. "No."

When I met some of our friends out in the courtyard, I told them of my misfortune and a girl who I had never met before, quite short compared to everyone else, with olive coloured skin and jet black hair that was in plaits, told me not to go away. A few minutes later she returned and produced a photo of Jennifer standing near the tall fir tree by the huts, her friend Amanda kneeling next to her. Although I didn't know where this girl had taken the photo from, maybe from Jennifer's collection, I was extremely grateful to her, and let's face it the photo was in good hands.

It didn't take me long to recognise Jennifer's brunette 'Bob' cut hairstyle. I always saw that in a crowd of girls long before I saw her and it gave me time to calm down before I began talking to her. She had that effect on me and the knot in my stomach still wouldn't go away. I wasn't naive enough to think I was the only boy in her life. I knew that one day she would leave the school and all this 'young love' would be gone, that added to my depression when I didn't see her and to my euphoria when I did—what a roller coaster life this was! I'm sure boys my age living in a street didn't have this problem with the 'girl next door' type of relationship, but I never could do anything the easy way and Jennifer was no girl next door.

For my pocket money I would mow the sports fields using the rusty old tractor the school had, along with its gang mowers, but they would often seize up due to too much grass getting caught. I would have to spend half-an-hour freeing them and it was one such afternoon I had to do this when one of the rollers slipped and the blades cut one of my fingers quite badly. I was in the middle of the sports field, but who should appear out of nowhere, Jennifer, ready to bandage my leaking finger.

"I do love you George, but my love will be of no use if you don't take care of yourself," she said as she put a daisy chain around my neck and gave me a kiss on the head.

Father had an old shed down the back drive, he used it for sharpening and storing motor mower parts and I was there one late sunny afternoon when I heard the voice of an angel. I had never heard such a voice before and had to check out who could sing so crystal clear, I should have known, sitting on her cloak spread out on a grassy bank and singing to a song she had composed herself was Jennifer. She was a very soft, kind girl, who always had a mystical air about her; she seemed far and away sometimes but didn't bat an eye lid as I intruded upon her. I was getting naughty thoughts about Jennifer, and I felt ashamed for she talked to me innocently about her songs and poems, and shared with me some snacks she had bought from the school tuck shop.

I really did want to put my arms around her and give her a hug and a kiss, she gave me a quick peck on the cheek then it was back to talking about her songs, I thought it was really lovely of her to ask my opinion as she sat there making the verses fit.

Her cloak was her sanctuary; I was told by our friends, if she asked you to share it, you really were someone special.

In an effort to get on with my life I joined the local Air Cadets, I was too young for a Foreign Legion. One week after joining we went on an exercise with the also local Sea Cadet Corps. Whilst our instructors escaped to a pub all night, the Sea Cadet instructors stayed with their boys. Theirs was a far better run outfit so it took me no time at all to join them, even if I didn't like the sea.

To keep fit we would challenge other groups to football matches. We had one such game against the Army Cadets. It was held on a freezing February, at night under floodlights. I was playing a strikers' role, the ball was coming over to me but high and out of the direct path of the floodlights, so much so that I lost track of it until it hit me in the groin, (that made me forget Jennifer)!

I was helped to the touchline, a man was pushing his way towards me, telling everyone he was a first aider, he said I needed to have a wee to keep the tubes open but I couldn't as I was empty. "Well can you masturbate?" That never came to me as an option, for only being twelve I didn't know what he meant, and I wasn't in the mood to do anything unusual by the side of a football pitch, especially in freezing cold weather and with four males stood over me.

Someone read my mind as they got rid of him. A few runs up and down the touchline and I went back on, only to find we were three goals down. Two of these were scored whilst I was off the pitch. I pulled two back, one a penalty and the other a header but we still lost three-two.

A few months later and we were off to a navy barracks in Dorset. As usual father was late getting me to the train station so I had to travel on my own. Luckily where I had to change trains the station staff just waved me through. When I arrived at the railway station at the end of my journey, the staff phoned the barracks for me, and out came some transport—a ten ton lorry for one little Sea Cadet and his kit bag.

At the barracks all my mates had bedded down and were in warm, well lit dorms, but there was no room for me. So a Petty Officer led me along a cinder track towards a tin hut. Inside were six matelots and a pop-belly stove, it was dark and cold but they made me some cocoa and we soon got chatting. They asked me if I wanted to eventually join the Navy, I told them I didn't know, they said if you do, don't trust the Officers, and if you become an Officer don't trust yourself. Away from the stove the hut was freezing; I couldn't sleep but duly attended to where we should muster the following morning, to go sailing. That was me and nobody else as my mates had decided to go to the local church and sing hymns where it would be warmer than out in a dinghy, they had forgotten to tell me.

I enjoyed the day sailing, everything that could be frozen off was! All I wanted to do now was to get home and see Jennifer.

I wasn't known for doing things by halves and the South East Sea Cadet cross country run was no exception. The competition took in Sussex, Surrey, Hampshire and Kent, a total of some eighty boys took part and as luck would have it, the run was being held in our area and was also the same route used by my school, so I was quite use to it. Cross country running was never my sport, I would always prefer to play football, but I felt I had to go along to give if only moral support to those who took it seriously.

I got round in what was good time for me, although I lost sight of the eight or so boys in front of me. I was quite pleased with my efforts, although the Chief Petty Officer threatened us with all sorts of punishments if we didn't win, especially on home turf. I thought I would leave that honour to my mates. As I was coming up to the finishing line, Chief was going crazy. He was urging me on as though I had won; he even greeted me with a slap on the back and said. "Well done." which I thought was taking the mickey a bit too far.

"Alright," I said. "Did any of us win it?"

"Yes you idiot," said the Chief. "You have."

"Very funny, there were eight in front of me, I couldn't see who they were, I just wondered if any of them were our lads."

"George," said Chief. "You had better get used to the idea of winning; because I'm telling you that you were first across the finishing line."

"But there will have to be a re-run," I protested. Then I saw the look of thunder on his face, he meant what he said I was the winner, what a joke.

Once we showered and were in uniform the medal ceremony was conducted with my name being read out, a quick march and salute to the Sub Lieutenant and I was given my medal. I felt I had cheated everyone who had taken part and when I got home I collected the usual sarcasm from father, "Were the rest in wheel chairs".

I threw the medal into the lake, it helped ease my guilty conscience, but the Corps had the last word as I had to have my photograph taken in the local paper. I told the C.O. I had given the medal to my granny in Portsmouth to look after, but our ship was given a medal as well so they used that.

Winning didn't stop there I was told to take my Leading Seaman's rank, which was fine by me, learning knots, navigation, sailing, rules of the sea and swimming, and the latter nearly being a disaster. I thought I had swum the required distance, but our local pool was smaller than some so I had to do another six lengths. This really affected my concentration and stamina as I only ever trained for what I thought was the right amount of lengths. As a result I caught cramp in my legs and I was going down for the third time out of my depth.

Yet again I heard a feint sound of a violin playing which got louder as my lungs were about to fill with water. I was going to drown but that did not happen. My head was being held out of the water giving enough time for one of my mates, Ian, to dive in and pull me out. After I had finished coughing and spluttering the Chief told me I was only six meters away from finishing and getting my Leading Seaman's rank, but. "Bad luck." He said: "You've got to do it all again, you've got an hour then you're back in that pool or else you've got me to answer to, do I make myself clear you miserable little man?"

I don't think he was looking for an answer, he was right if I had stayed out I would have lost my nerve.

As I sat on the side of the pool still catching my breath Ian came and sat beside me. I thanked him for his help. He gave me a quizzical look and said: "How did you do it?"

"How did I do what?"

"You're the only person I know, that has cramp in the legs and can still tread water, if you hadn't done that I couldn't have saved you."

I didn't answer him, simply because I couldn't, I didn't know what had kept my head above water. I had to think seriously about the violin I could hear. The music started off quiet which warned me that danger was close, and then it got louder as the danger was imminent, disappearing altogether when the danger had passed. I went back into the pool to show myself I was no fraud, and went on and completed the required lengths.

There was a five-a-side football competition being held at Portsmouth for the Sea Cadets, as with the cross country run the same units went along. We were warming up when two Cadets came over to me. They were big lads for their age. One said: "Hello Mr cross country winner, you won't be cheating your way to this medal."

Then both walked off, I could have explained but they didn't look the sort who would have believed me if I did. My mates gathered round me to find out what the conversation was all about, but I kept quiet as I didn't want us to be here for all the wrong reasons.

We were at the quarter-final stage late in the afternoon when, of all the luck, we were drawn against the team that those two lads were in. I scored the only goal just as they were about to tackle me. That was a joke, one raked my right shin as the other elbowed me in the face, blood everywhere (mine). The ref didn't see it but my mates were going mad. That was the end of my day and we were knocked out in the next round.

Back home without asking me what had happened father kept up his ritual of forming his own opinion of me. "Look at you, you just can't keep your big mouth shut can you, I told you someone would shut it for you one day." How perceptive of him.

From the navy barracks in Portsmouth I watched the drab concrete jungle being built that was to be the new shopping centre. I found the city depressing enough, this just added to it. We visited the barracks on several occasions to get us into the Navy way of life and to go sailing and learn navigation, plus the odd visit to Clarence pier.

This visit was to learn chart work in the bowels of a fishing vessel whilst steaming around the Solent, that's what my mates did. I sat astern nibbling on half a loaf of bread given to me by the stoker who I left puzzled as to why I joined the Cadets, if I felt so queasy on board.

The Sea Cadet Corp had an island in the middle of the Thames near Hammersmith. We would often go there for rowing practice and dinghy sailing. It was also good fun to learn capsize drill, and we soon learnt that power does not give way to sail, well not on the Thames.

At night everything had to be ship shape. All ropes on board dinghies and on shore had to be coiled flat so that when you trod on them it was like treading on a mat. This was not done just to look good it also prevented anyone tripping and maybe falling into the water. We could go for a row on our own in small boats called ducklings. They were awkward little boats and the rower could be prone to 'catching a crab,' that is the tide takes away one of your oars, and this happened to one of my mates. He was left stranded with a Thames cruiser bearing down on him. As luck would have it an instructor was nearby in a canoe and dragged him out of the way with seconds to spare.

Going there was for a week at a time, just as you were getting use to the place it was time to leave. Still it was back home to the school and my beloved girlfriend Jennifer—in my dreams as the saying goes.

CHAPTER 6

This Saturday afternoon was one of those hot afternoons where trying to do the most minuscule of tasks took the greatest effort. I therefore decided I was going to read my book in the orchard sitting on a car rug under the shade of a tree full of Granny Smiths. As I crossed the drive that separated our house from the orchard I had to put everything back indoors as I had caught sight of the Drama teacher Miss Cornford, alone in the orchard. That started alarm bells ringing as she was never seen that far away from her beloved flower borders and standing alone in the orchard she somehow looked so out of place.

As I walked towards this lovely old dear, I could see tears running down her heavy make-up, again something alien to me. She was a grand old lady, probably in her late seventies, and I thought she had seen and done it all. I'm sure tears didn't come easy, which made me fear the worst. I knew I had to comfort her, she would have expected that, but I had never put my arms around a woman before, let alone a grand old lady like her. Even when Karen was dumped and crying I left her to it. This was going to be a real effort on my behalf and I put an arm around her shoulders which she thanked me for, saying. "Willies died."

"I'm sorry to hear that." Not having a clue who she was talking about.

"Will you bury him for me? I have taken a spade from out of the shed and I will show you where I want him placed."

I'm glad she kept talking; it gave me a chance to figure out who Willy was. Of course, it was one of two Poodles that accompanied Miss Joyce and Miss Cornford everywhere.

We walked out of the orchard and past the flower beds towards the patio where the grand French windows of the drawing room opened, leaving the scent from the adjacent rose boarder to waft in. I listened to her reminiscing about Willy, from what she said he certainly lived to a ripe old age.

"Here we are, just here." She indicated a hard, bare piece of ground between the rose boarder and the patio. Today of all days in this heat! Oh well. I began digging away, it was certainly hard going, but I suppose it would give her some comfort to know Willy would be just outside from where she worked at her desk, along with Miss Joyce.

I didn't realise at the time that Jerry, the other poodle had already died and I do wish the dear lady had told me this was the exact same spot where Jerry had been planted for whilst digging, I kept thinking Willy would have loved these bones. After an hour in the blistering heat I had finished the job and he was at rest.

As I made my way to the shed to return the spade I saw a girl sitting on some stone steps that led up to the main lawn. I had seen her before on a couple of occasions, organising everyone about, but I had never got the chance to speak to her. She had long black hair in ringlets, quite slim and she was wearing the summer dress which was short sleeved, white with thin green horizontal stripes. I stood looking at her, waiting for her to look up, but she was miles away reading a book which was in the lap of her dress, kept there by her legs, which were a bit too far apart, she was twiddling her hair with the fingers on her left hand.

I had to consider if I was being set up again, but decided to make a comment. I always liked to break the ice with the girls if only to reassure them that I wasn't some kind of letch, and after all she was supposed to be a young lady!

"Do you know you're showing your unmentionables?" I said.

Without moving or looking up she said. "That's what I call my grandmother's knickers, don't be so rude dear boy."

"I'm not being rude I just thought you would like to know."

Once she had finished reading her page she closed her book with her knees, and gave me a look that said I've got the devil in me, and she wasn't joking.

"Most boys wouldn't have commented. They would have kept me talking and hoped I didn't move. What's the matter didn't you like what you were gawping at? Anyway what have you been doing you stink?"

"I've just buried the last Poodle."

"About time too, I for one kept lacing its food, don't look so surprised, you didn't have to put up with it, all it did was wee, yap and crap."

She rose and walked towards me. "Go and have a bath before you give the place a bad name." I'm almost sure she only meant to give me a playful slap on the face, but lacrosse and swimming must have given her muscles she didn't know she had, as she nearly took my head off. "That's for looking at my pants."

No introduction was needed, Amanda told me her sister would be here this term. "She's very feisty," were her words. Yes; I have just met Natasha, Amanda wasn't wrong.

She walked away from me for a few yards and slowly turned around to face me. "Look," she said. "We seemed to have got off on the wrong foot, did I hurt you?"

"No you didn't, although I do seem to have a twitch in my left eye that wasn't there before."

"Well it serves you right, now come on lets be friends. I'll tell you what; I'll give you a chance to redeem yourself."

"Thank you," I said. "That's very kind of you."

"Are you any good with your hands?"

"I don't want to be that friendly."

"I can always put a twitch in the other eye; would you be able to put up some pictures by the side of my bed?"

"Yes, I've always been allowed to roam the dorms as I please, even more so when you girls are here." I replied sarcastically. She looked at me as though all hope had gone. "There are plenty of builders here, I did approach one of the men but he was far too busy. Anyway just walk around like you own the place, no one will be any the wiser. I'm in Bluebell dorm first on the left. I'll leave some pins on the bed for you, be a dear for me?"

"I'll think about it."

"I haven't really hurt you have I?" She said as a smile crept across her face. Even if she had, the answer would still have been the same. "No, no you haven't."

Well I thought, as first meetings go that was a disaster.

I watched her walk away and couldn't help thinking; if she's like this at thirteen what will she be like at double the age, some man is going to have one hell of a roller coaster life with her.

A few hours later and her job was completed, her pictures were of her, Amanda, mum and dad, complete with a massive house of about ten bedrooms, staff, horses, and swimming pool, you name it. Somewhere hot and abroad. I dare say Natasha was use to getting her own way, what a handful she was going to be—although I did enjoy the banter between us.

Word soon got round about my handiwork in the dormitory. On Monday afternoon after school I decided to do some fishing but it came to an abrupt halt as Jeff, one of the builders asked me to help him on the flat roof over the walkway that ran between the gym and part of the changing rooms where the girls kept their games boots in the wire cages. I liked Jeff he was an old boy who smoked a pipe. He always had time for people, and if you wanted to know what he was doing he would stop and explain, not shoo you away like some of them.

"As you impersonate us, I thought you wouldn't mind giving me a hand."

"Not at all, who told you?"

"I popped up to the dorm this morning. I'm the only one here today, that's why I need your help, I guessed you had done it for her over the week-end, nice lass isn't she?" Yes, I thought, she's certainly a character.

As I climbed the ladder in the warm sunshine, I could hear the classroom to my right was in session, the adjacent one was empty and I could hear Amanda playing her violin. It was her tell tale music, which surprised me as the music room was well insulated.

At the top of the ladder I looked around at the school grounds, the tennis courts, the drive and the games fields, the peace and quiet. I felt a warm feeling surround me. I went to leave the ladder—I couldn't, something was preventing me, along with Amanda's violin I immediately realised what was happening. I called to Jeff to stay where he was, I shouted at him to a point where a teacher appeared from the classroom and told me to be quiet.

He looked back at me as I carried on shouting at him not to go any further. "I've repaired lots of roofs in my time, it's perfectly safe," he said, as he disappeared from view. I didn't hear him hit the concrete walkway below as pieces of joisting and dusty old roofing felt followed him down with a loud crashing noise.

The power that had kept me fixed to the ladder released me, I scrambled down to see if I could put my sea cadet first aid training to good use, but he was beyond that as blood was pouring from his head.

I checked all the known places for a pulse but there wasn't one, so I put my coat over him least some young girl gets her first sight of a corpse, and ran to the secretary's office to phone for an ambulance.

Fortunately all the teachers fearing the worst kept the girls in their classrooms, until one teacher ventured out; Fiona the English teacher. She was very slim, about 30—years-old, with short auburn hair wearing a green twinset (well that's how mother described them) and a black skirt. I told her of the tragedy, she was very sympathetic and offered to help, but I told her the ambulance was on its way. Sadly when it arrived the paramedic agreed with my diagnosis, and then took Jeff away.

I sat down in the walkway near where Jeff had died and began to cry, mainly as a result of shock more than anything else. I could see along the classrooms that overlooked the courtyard and saw Amanda leaving the music room, my guardian angel. Natasha was walking across the courtyard towards the clock tower exit. She caught sight of me and came over, obviously not knowing what had taken place. "Thanks for doing my pictures; cheer up anyone would think someone has just died judging by the look on your face." I walked her away from the scene and told her I would see her later.

A bucket of water washed what was left of Jeff down a nearby drain. He died as a result of not knowing some builders had started stripping away some of the joists and roofing felt. They had re-covered it all on the Friday night to resume on Monday but had been called away. Nobody had told this to Jeff and they had made such a good job of covering their work for the weekend, it was hardly noticeable and that's where Jeff had fallen through. Had I been the first on the roof I may well have been in the ambulance instead of him.

I looked at my coat and decided there had been enough of other people's bodily fluids in it, and where they had been washed off in the swimming pool the chlorine was starting to eat away the cotton stitching. The incinerator was alight so that's where I dumped it.

On my way out of the courtyard curiosity got the better of me. I went to the music room and saw that all the acoustic tiles had been removed prior to the workmen refurbishing the room, I would therefore have heard Amanda's violin whether she was playing it as part of her practice or sending me a warning, now I was totally confused.

I walked off towards the lake to try and take my mind off what I had just witnessed, and to try and make some sense of it all. I sat down at my usual place and looked out over the lake. So totally absorbed in my own thoughts was I that I didn't hear little miss sweetheart approach, the love of my life Jennifer. She had written me a poem and as she read it I began to forget the trauma of the past hour and was being filled with her and everything she said. When she had finished her poem she gave me a piece of pottery, it was inscribed with the word 'Jennifer', it had a jagged edge down one side. She said it was one half of a heart and she had the other half with a jagged edge that interlocked with my half, and was inscribed with the word 'George'.

She really was a very sweet romantic girl and I loved her for it. She said, "All the time we have our pottery hearts we will never be apart." When she responded to my kiss it sent my ego sky high. I felt our vibes filled with warm tender love being transferred between us, I felt the tight knot together with erupting stomach acid disappear, for now, I knew it would all return the moment we had to part. Somehow I wanted more than just love to keep us together. I was starting to feel really possessive towards her, although I should be thankful for the school for bringing us both together, I also began to feel a certain resentment as the school took up most of her time.

As I arrived home I knew no one had heard about Jeff, as father greeted me with. "As you don't have a brother this must be for you, Miss Cornford stopped by this afternoon." He handed me an envelope which had a hand-written letter inside and a ten shilling note, he also handed me a box of chocolates that she had also left for me.

He continued: "I don't know what you have done to deserve all that, I take it you've done something right for once."

"I buried Willie for her." I showed him the note that said how kind and understanding I had been, I've never seen him look so miserable. I was in his good books for as long as it took me to tell him Jeff had died and how he had died. On that he saw his chance to even the score, criticising my efforts to save Jeff, and reminding me that wherever I was, trouble was never far behind. I knew I could never base an argument on Amanda warning me with her violin and preventing me from leaving the ladder. He was therefore convinced that constantly finding fault with me was the right thing to do.

The following evening I entered Natasha's classroom to sweep it, she was there with twelve other girls gathered around the record player.

"Hello dear boy," she said. This was the usual way she greeted me. "What's this man singing about? He sings about a house in the American deep south, New Orleans." "Why, do you want a job there?" I said.

"Is it the sort of place I would go for a job then?" She replied.

She really didn't know what this song was all about, I wasn't being set up. This is going to even the score from the other day I thought, when some little gem from around the other side of the desk said. "No it's a brothel." I just managed to shut the door behind me when I heard something hit it with a thud, then the language from a young lady! "I'LL MAKE SURE YOU'RE OF

NO BLOODY USE IN ONE IF YOU EVER COME NEAR ME AGAIN; BASTARD." The trouble was the more she lost her temper the more I laughed uncontrollably, with tears running down my face.

The following evening I met one of her friends in the courtyard, Keira, she was quite small for her age and a bit of a swat, I could always rely on her to tell me the truth. "I really upset Natasha last night." I said.

"No you didn't, she thinks you're great fun, she said in the dorm last night, he got one over on me the bastard, I hate him, then started laughing. She loves it if people stand up to her and give as good as they get."

She squeezed my arm as she left. That's as maybe I thought, but all this boisterous behaviour will sooner or later come to the attention of a teacher and I could be banned from visiting the school. No contest, I wasn't going to put at risk never seeing Jennifer again.

CHAPTER 7

"When are you going to take me to see United?" This is the question Karen greeted me with one morning. My reply was well thought out, full of tact, I was at my diplomatic best and executed it to perfection. "I'm not," I replied.

"Oh gone on, my treat."

"Go on your own."

"I can't, you know the London Underground, and I don't," she wailed.

"You don't know a thing about football, and you will be asking me silly girlie questions all through the match, find someone else to go with." Mother didn't help. "She is offering to pay George, go on take her."

Father waded in. "She better not come to any harm George, if there's a fight and she gets hurt I will hold you responsible."

Somebody please save me from sisters and parents; I don't want to take her, I have no intention of fighting with anyone and if it all goes wrong it's my fault, I'm really going to look forward to this. "Why do you want to go and see United of all teams?" "I want to see their new striker, the one with the long black hair and gorgeous legs, I think he's lovely, and I know you would take me because they're your team." Oh well it looked like I had been lumbered.

"They are down in London on Good Friday, will that do?"

"Will he be playing?"

"Well yes as I pick the team I'll put him in the side just for you." "There's no need for sarcasm, talk to your sister properly," said father.

I left the house thinking this lot could start an argument in an empty room. I went off towards the lake for some sanity; I think I had earned it. As I walked along the drive just past the gym some girls were leaving the lacrosse pitch. I didn't realise I knew most of them—they looked different in sports gear.

Amanda came up and started talking to me. As I listened to her I immediately thought, where there is Amanda there is Jennifer, so I searched around for the tell tale page boy hair style, hoping to get a peep of her sexy legs in a short games skirt, and there she was standing right at the back of all the girls. Jennifer could change her character to suite the situation, feminine and romantic when we were alone but absolutely devastating when I couldn't touch her. This was one of those occasions. Standing there alone letting me absorb the moment to its greatest impact, her tousled hair, firm breasts shaping her thin games shirt, her slender mud-covered thighs and holding her broken lacrosse stick.

I could only admire the performance she was putting on for me, when I looked at her she was smouldering and there wasn't a thing I could do about it. With a wink of her eye she came running up to me and gave me a quick peck on the cheek. "And where are you off to?" She asked.

"Off to the lake, I've just about had enough of people to—day." I then told her about the football match Karen wanted to go to. Her head dropped as she didn't want me to go, warning me there could be trouble. "I wouldn't have told you if I knew it would upset you," I said.

"No," she said. "I'm glad you told me. You just need looking after that's all."

The coming football match and all the troubles it brought me didn't seemed to matter right now because Jennifer was pulling out a tissue from her green games knickers, sending my temperature soaring. All these things are so matter of fact for girls, not giving a second's thought to what it's doing to a young boy, who can only pretend it doesn't matter.

Good Friday came round far too quick. I couldn't look fed up and take Karen's money so I decided to treat her instead. On the train going to London every time I looked at her she was beaming with excitement.

At the ground I made my way to the turnstile. There was an elderly man at the barrier; he seemed to talk through his nose so it was quite difficult to understand him.

I said, "Two tickets please."

He replied, "Are you taking the piss?"

"No," I answered. "I would like to pay for two tickets."

"You are; you're taking the piss."

"Look," I said. "What is the problem?"

"The problem, I'll give you problem, it's all-ticket you wanker, now piss off before I call the Police."

Helpful chap, I wonder how he got his nasal problem.

I turned to where Karen was waiting. "It's an all ticket game," I said.

"What does that mean?"

Shut up George, count to ten. I did and I still couldn't help myself. "I would hazard a guess and say it means we've got to have a ticket."

"Didn't you know that?"

I could either put up with the bloke at the barrier or Karen, but I really couldn't put up with both of them.

I said, "I'm very sorry, it's a hard lesson learned, but we will just have to go home."

Shame as it was a brilliant sunny day. As we turned away a man I wouldn't buy a box of matches from said, "You looking for tickets for the game? How many do you want? Two, two tickets here you are."

"How much?"

I saw that they were marked up at ten shillings each, so I expected to pay a lot more than that. "Face value," he said. "That'll be a quid."

I handed over the pound; I thought I've got to waste a pound for Karen's sake.

To Karen this was like going to a cup final, it was her first football match. I prepared her for the worst: "Look Karen no way are these real tickets, this is a United game and tickets will be like gold dust. We'll try and go through with them, but we are going to be called back and thrown out, but we might as well give it a go."

"O.k." she said. We made our way to the turnstile where 'happy' was, he took the tickets from me and gave me back the stubs and released the turnstile for us to pass through. I was bracing myself for the man to realise the tickets were forgeries, and for the police to be looking for us, but it never happened, we were in.

We placed ourselves halfway back from the pitch and along one of the sides. United were two goals up in no time. Her idol had scored both of them and Karen was going mad, then he scored a third, I got caught up in Karen's excitement and started to wave my scarf about and cheer, when a man leaned over me and said: "If you wave that scarf in my face once more I'm going to choke you with it".

Oh dear, I had a sister to look after so I had to accept the threat and behave, then the atmosphere around us was broken with: "Don't you talk to my brother like that, just because your crappy team are losing."
Did I hear right? "Was that you?" I said.
"Well you ought to learn to stick up for yourself."
Before she could say anymore the thug she yelled at politely whispered in my ear. "I'll be looking for you after the game. I'll teach you to let that little slag talk to me like that." I looked around so I knew who was going to send me to my maker and saw that this Neanderthal was with a group of about fifteen like-minded thugs.

"Oh wonderful," I said to Karen. "You've just landed me with a nightmare, how do I get us home in one piece?"

"What are we going to do George? I'm really scared." To make matters worse United went on to win four nil.

We managed to get out of the ground and saw some Police Officers managing crowd control, I went to explain our problem but the Officer shouted right in my face. "MOVE ALONG NOW."

I said to Karen, "This is no good the Police are far too busy, and in any case they cannot escort the two of us to Victoria Station from here." We made our way to the nearest underground station but our 'friends' were already there and they were not catching a train.

"They have cut us off from getting a train," I told Karen. "We will just have to walk."

At this point we were joined by some more supporters of our age. They had been threatened with violence and were just as frightened, and they had to get to Victoria station so we let them walk with us.

As we were walking along some of the other supporters began to argue about the right way to go, they walked away from us, but Karen wanted to be with them so we had to follow. The route we were taking was leading us to some high rise flats. It was here I heard the feint sound of a violin playing. "I'm turning back," I said to the others. "It's not safe." They argued but when they saw me walking away they followed. The violin was still playing but getting louder. I felt sure Amanda was watching over us.

"How do you know it's not safe?" One of them asked me, he was a tall, skinny lad and had a problem with acne and bad breath. His friends called him Shag, not a name I would have given him. I only had time to say. "Quick, behind this lorry."

We all ducked down just in time to see the thugs that had threatened us walk by.

I heard one say, "They're around here somewhere, they're not making for Euston Station to go north I've checked, so they must be going to Victoria, we'll have 'em."

That really scared all of us; these thugs were now carrying baseball bats and broken bottles. "Can we stay with you?" asked Shag. "Yes," I said. "But no more arguing, you do as I say, is that clear?" They all nodded in agreement.

One thing's for sure I can always bank on Karen's help in a situation like this. "I can't believe you brought me to this game, these people are really nasty."
"It was you who told them they had a crappy team." "Well fathers going to be livid with you if anything happens to me."

We reached Victoria Station. We were on the main concourse looking at the departure board when one of our group shouted: "LOOK WHAT YOU'VE LEAD US INTO YOU BLOODY FOOL, WHY DID WE EVER LISTEN TO YOU?"

We saw the thugs running towards us, empty broken beer bottles had already started to rain down on us. Women and children were running and screaming in all directions, but these thugs had done their homework—there was nowhere for us to run to. One of our group was bleeding from the head after being struck by a bottle.

As they closed in swearing and telling us what they were going to do, I became confused, the violin music was not playing at all, not even a feint sound, which would have put me on my guard, nothing. It was Karen who shouted. "LOOK." I turned around and all became clear. I could not believe my eyes; I have never seen so many German Shepherd dogs before, together with their Police handlers they were a welcome sight.

The thugs took off leaving us to catch our train, with the dogs snapping and snarling at their heels.

When we got home Karen told mother and father about the day and how I nearly got her killed. That started father off. "You just cannot keep out of trouble can you? Well she will not be going with you again." Amen to that I thought.

It was term time again and in the evenings I went looking for the love of my life Jennifer, I soon discovered that Jennifer was different to the other girls, and that you didn't pick Jennifer as a friend, she chose you.

My appearance at a classroom was now predictable. As soon as I appeared one of the girls would disappear to find Jennifer for me. She was an elusive lass and soon there would be girls telling me where they saw her last. The trouble is they would be telling me all at once, which was quite a noise making their information of no use, but with young girls the thought that they were caught up in a budding romance was too much of a temptation for them. Not wanting to be left out, a dozen girls would go looking for her, some shouting out her name, and I wanted to keep things quiet and have her all to myself, some chance. When I felt I could take this embarrassment no longer I would tell Amanda I was leaving.

I headed for the lake to where I had a fishing rod hidden in a hollowed-out tree. In no time I was watching the float bobbing about, but feeling a bit down that despite the girls' efforts no one could find Jennifer. It was good to have the girls on my side. They were caught up in all the intrigue and could go to places to find her where I didn't want to make a habit of going, like dormitories. Whilst these thoughts were going through my head a rustle of some bushes by the foot path would make me aware that I had company. I looked along the path and could only make out a pair of bare legs, one of the girls I dare say telling me what I already knew, they couldn't find her.

The noise soon became a sight and what a sight, I couldn't believe my eyes for stood there was the gorgeous Jennifer. I didn't really know what to say to her which was nothing unusual as I was always a bundle of nerves in her presence, so I came out with the obvious. "There are girls out looking for you." She just smiled at me and shrugged her pretty little shoulders; my ego was up in the heavens. Jennifer had taken the trouble to come and find me, and just as I thought nothing could better this she unclasped her school cloak and laid it on the ground for both of us to sit on. I did notice that she was wearing her school uniform, the flimsy summer dress, which on her was quite short; I thought to myself she is not going to be able to sit on the cloak without showing 'everything'.

As I thought the world of her I looked out over the lake until she had made herself comfortable. I knew a cheeky peek would have been well on the cards, but a well educated girl such as Jennifer would have appreciated my respect for her, after all I did want to see her again; a far more rewarding prospect than seeing what else she was wearing.

We were soon sitting side by side when suddenly Jennifer edged herself towards me and cuddled my left arm. Could a moment in time be any better than this? In my eyes the answer was no. As I held my fishing rod I felt the line go tight and the float disappeared, who cares, nothing was going to spoil this. I knew this was going to be an afternoon I was never going to forget. Times like these would be few and far between so now I just savoured the moment. As I laid on her cloak she propped herself up on one arm looking over me, then she went for it, kissing me like mad on my neck, which sent shivers up and down my spine making me laugh uncontrollably.

* * *

"Want to come for a sail?" said father. It was the summer holidays and he didn't want me hanging about the place fretting because the girls had gone home.

"Where to?" I said.

"France, Cherbourg, you can tell your chief you navigated your way over the channel, that would be a feather in your cap for your next promotion."

Not the way we do it, I thought.

Here we go twenty hours of boredom. Father would have gone by himself; such was his love of the sea, this always worried mother. "One day the Police will be knocking on our door and I shall fear the worst, go with him George," she pleaded. "Keep him out of trouble."

A week away from home it was then. We loaded the boat the following morning. Father had brought her round to the jetty which saved a trudge through the mud. We left on the afternoon tide, nothing like a few hours notice that you were going away for a week.

We only had the engine running as there was no wind, just a very hot sunny afternoon as we headed towards the Isle of Wight. I could see a black dot in the sky off our starboard bow and wondered what it could be. In no time at all the dot turned into a Spitfire. I loved the sound of the Merlin engines, purring, as the pilot banked away, in response to my wave he waggled the wings of the plane and was gone, what a superb way to start a voyage.

My twenty hours of the journey would be in the cockpit, I couldn't go below as that would start off the 'avoir le mal de mer' and it wouldn't stop till we reached France.

Four hours on, four hours off, meant I shifted from one seat to steer, and another to try and get some sleep. That was a joke, every so often some spray from the sea swells would wake me up with a start and it wasn't long before I was begging for some proper shut eye, but we had a long way to go.

"It's your turn at the tiller." I didn't need rousing I was already awake. Father brought me a cup of tea before turning in, his snoring made me so envious.

We were entering the shipping lanes—not so much a problem where we were crossing. There had been a severe storm in the Channel last night but right now the sea was as calm as a mill pond which still meant putting up with the noise of the engine rather than the swish and crack of the sails. With my level of alertness that was probably just as well as the boat could steer itself on the auto helm. I hung onto the tiller more as decoration so that we didn't quite look like the Marie Celeste.

After what seemed forever, but actually about an hour, I was woken by a stiff breeze, which also made the sea more lively—time to hoist the sails I thought. With the following sea we could go all the way to Cherbourg on this tack, going about every so often to counter the distance the tide would have taken us off course.

Sailing held my interest for so long but I still let the auto helm do most of the work. Despite 'going like a rocket', having little to do I soon dozed off again.

Suddenly I was jolted into a state of alertness and confusion, the sails were flapping and the boom was crossing from side to side at an alarming rate, the boat wanted to alter course on its own. I checked the auto helm, the stud holding the arm to the tiller had sheared off. That would have taken more strength than I could imagine. No matter what I tried the boat seemed to have a mind of its own making.

I was left to wrestle with the tiller, but it was of no use. I was thrown across the cockpit in my attempt to keep her on course and at the same time I heard the sound of a violin playing very loudly. The heavens opened up with rain lashing down on me, something did not want me in the cockpit.

I worked like mad only to be thrown around, receiving cuts and bruises for my troubles. It was as if something was trying to shake me off the tiller and with the auto helm out of action I checked the compass for a bearing. To my astonishment it was spinning like a top.

All this commotion had finally woken father, I heard a familiar growl of. "George what the heck do you think you're doing?"

Without the help of the compass I had to give the boat its head. I watched in amazement as the bows came round, I looked at the compass. It had stopped spinning round and showed we were fifteen degrees off our original course. I listened for the tell tale violin but everything was quiet.

The boat seemed quite content now she was heading in a new direction still at a vast rate of knots, leaving me to explain something that was a complete mystery. Father came into the cockpit still upset from being woken prematurely.

"Well what was that all about?" He growled.

"I've no idea."

"You've disabled the auto helm and fell on the tiller in your sleep," he said all simplistically.

"The auto . . ." but before I could finish father was looking through binoculars from the stern out at sea on the course we should have been on. "Drop the sails and motor back the way we came George, the waves are breaking over something that I need to take a look at."

I did as I was asked. "Right slow her down and turn to starboard. Praise to god and all that is holy." I heard him say, when I heard that I knew father had been humbled.

Through the binoculars he could clearly make out several sea containers bobbing up and down with the waves, probably ones that fell overboard during last night's storm and he went on half mumbling to himself. "If we had hit those at our speed we would have holed and sunk in no time at all. I wouldn't even have had time to get off a May Day. In this water we would have barely lasted a few minutes."

"You can't be sure," I said.

"Yes I can", he replied, full of confidence. "I saw this happen to a yacht in the Solent. As it happens they were relatives of a family that your mother and I used to work for, Commander Rubens and his wife. The tragedy happened to their daughter and her family but they were only in the water for a short while. We were the nearest boat and when we fished them out they were all dead. This was the boating accident that caused us to have to move from Farthings in Portsmouth".

I don't know what you had in mind just now George but you've just saved our lives. I had my own theory on this but I don't think father would ever take me seriously again if I told him what it was.

Instead all I could manage was. "The auto helm broke during the struggle." He missed the point and said that would have been the least of our worries. There was no convincing him that something had altered our course and it was none of my doing. Even just as strange, now that we had passed the containers, I was able to put the boat back on our original course without any trouble.

That near miss was a wake-up call. I looked around to see what safety equipment if any, there was. "Do we have a tender?" I asked.

Father indicated a collapsible boat, a heap of plastic and plywood lashed to the top of the cabin. I would really love to put that together in a hurry! I'm sure it was the ideal transport in a marina, but given a rough sea it probably wouldn't be worth undoing it from the cabin roof.

I poked around in some lockers and found what looked like dynamite in one of them. "What are these?"
"They're flares."
"Are they?"
"Well I bought them from a boat jumble."
"And that qualifies them as flares does it?" I asked.
"Well they're better than nothing," he snapped.
"Have you ever lit one to see what they do?"
"No, but when or if the time comes I'm sure they will be alright so don't concern yourself."

"It might be me that has to light one." I said. "If I do I want it to say help me I'm in trouble, I don't want a round of applause for a firework display."

That did it. My father can be Le sulk when he wants to be. I learned from him that sulking is a complete waste of an emotion. It looks juvenile and stops any differences from being solved. My way was always to talk things through, no matter how painful.

I kept on talking to him because I wasn't going to have a long silence from now until we reached Cherbourg. Like a dog at a bone I kept gnawing away until I heard from the cabin. "Do you want a hand with the sails?"
Hurrah. "No you go to sleep."
"You will have to pay attention from now on; you have no auto helm to rely on."
"I know," I said. "The stud sheared off holding it onto the tiller."
"But that would have taken a strength of Herculean proportions." He said. He shrugged his shoulders and went back to his bunk, not that interested, but then he wasn't in the cockpit when it happened.

What going to sea was all about was seeing two dolphins playing with our trailing log, taking it in turns to flick it out of the water, now that did keep me awake. Father had some mackerel to use as bait so I threw it to them.

I know they are perfectly capable of catching their own fish but I liked watching them leaping and twisting out of the water, catching what I threw before it hit the waves.

To me though this added to the mystery that dolphins appeared soon after a narrow escape with death. Maybe they had been summoned to the area as a backup should the first life saving act have failed, after all at sea they were man's best friend!

As we neared Cherbourg a thought crossed my mind that maybe I was going to spend the week sleeping in order to be fit for the return voyage. On looking around, the town had plenty of wartime memorabilia which would certainly keep me occupied for a week. Father preferred some sea fishing.

Despite the stories I had listened to I found the French people to be friendly, they were very tolerant when I tried to make myself understood. Again something strange happened to me. I was about to cross a busy road and would have walked into the path of a car as it was being driven far too fast round a sharp bend. I had forgotten that abroad driving is on the right and as I stepped into the path of the car I was hauled back onto the pavement.

I had buckled up the belt of my jacket around the back. I stood too near some iron railings and the buckle had caught up in them. I thought at first someone had pulled me back, but then realised what had happened. I still found it absurd that this had happened by chance, but as no one else was around I had to accept it.

Like all holidays this one was over in no time. Not because the week was up, but my thoughtful father had studied the weather forecast. If I was to be got home in one piece it was best to leave as soon as possible.

Once out at sea, according to father I was going to get a real French treat, a ham sandwich like no other, real thick granary bread, equally thick sliced local ham; topped with French mustard; a real door stop of a sandwich. I sunk my teeth into this delight and spat it into the sea. "That tastes like shit."

He looked absolutely crest fallen at my description of his efforts. "What was in that?" I asked. "Ham and mustard" was the reply.

He took a bite out of his own sandwich and agreed it tasted dreadful, he opened it and said. "Oh blast."

I had to really push him to find out what 'oh blast' meant; when he did tell me I wish I hadn't asked. Whilst in Cherbourg, amongst other things he had bought two tubes, one was a tube of mustard and the other was a tube of haemorrhoid cream. Out came the excuses, I can't read French; it was dark in the cabin. Whatever, it would not have been good for my stomach at the start of a long journey had I swallowed it.

I was coping quite well with the effect the boat had on me as it 'corkscrewed' through the waves, maybe I was getting use to this sailing lark after all. I even felt peckish after missing out on my sandwich. It was father's turn to take the tiller so I asked him if he had anything to eat that was close to hand. He hadn't, but offered to go and make me something, that made me cry out a loud. "NO, it doesn't matter." I didn't want the saga of the pile cream again.

He then searched through his pockets and produced a chunk of date loaf and handed it to me. I don't like dates and I had no idea how long this had been in his pocket but I was hungry, so I took the risk. Only when it hit my stomach did I taste the diesel that had permeated this offering and, as if my stomach was a trampoline, it all bounced straight back up again.

The night sky had drawn in by the time I had stopped being ill, dawn had broken by the time I woke up. I found I had a rope tied around my waist; the other end was secured inside the cockpit. "You wanted to chuck yourself overboard," was father's explanation. My chest and stomach are in so much pain due to retching when you've nothing to bring up except your main organs, I could well believe him.

CHAPTER 8

As we were nearing the Isle of Wight we met the sailor's worst nightmare, heavy fog. From now on whatever lights or buoys that suddenly greeted us out of this murky cloak meant nothing, a couple of meters vision off the bow and that was our lot.

After another hour of moving into the unknown, the fog seemed to become denser. We could hear people talking and the metallic noises that would come from a ship. Something was telling me not to go on. I suggested that we should drop anchor before we discovered where the noise was coming from. I remained on watch with a cup of tea as company whilst father got a well-earned sleep from doing a double shift, due to my incapacitation.

My grandmother on my father's side had always maintained we were a family of dormice and I did nothing to prove her wrong. When I eventually woke up from keeping watch I immediately solved the mystery of all the shouting and general noise that had been hidden by the fog, the fog that had so suddenly become denser than ever before and I could see now in the clear light of day why a voice from somewhere was shouting at me to drop anchor. No more than eighty meters off our bows was an Aircraft Carrier, like us at anchor.

I roused father to come and look at this fantastic sight. He had to rub his eyes twice as he couldn't believe what he saw first time. He had brought his camera with him for the trip and photographed every nut, bolt and rivet that kept the ship together. He wanted me in the pictures but I could feel how matted and sticky out my hair was, this together with my best sea sick look, left me to convince father I would not enhance his photos.

Two rolls of film later we were moving on. Whilst I was steering, father was below cooking eggs and bacon. He did offer some to me but not wishing to wake up the gremlins in my stomach I declined, deciding to let sleeping dogs lie.

It wasn't long before we were in the sanctuary of Chichester harbour. The tide and wind were against us so we had to use motor and sail to make any headway. We were doing fine. I was enjoying the calmer waters of the harbour, but all had to go wrong, if not life gets boring!

"That boat's run aground," said father. "On a falling tide as well, they will be there for hours, let's see if we can tow them off." They accepted our offer. "This is awfully decent of you." said one of the men. "We would probably be here all night waiting for the tide to return."

I secured our rope around their mast, and we were just motoring off when I shouted. "Rope in the water." Too late, around the prop it went, stopping our engine dead. It was very thoughtful of father to hand me the knife, and even more thoughtful that whilst I was cutting the rope free he was trying to start the engine. Luckily for me he failed in the attempt, as soon as I was out of the water the engine started first time.

"Right," said father. "I'm going to coil the rope in the cockpit and pay it out as we go, that way we won't have rope all over the place getting caught up in anything. You look after the throttle." Father shouted out a reassuring. "Be with you in a minute." He could see the concerned look on the faces of the people we were supposed to be rescuing.

I moved the boat off gently as father payed out the rope. We had come to the limit of our tow rope and it was going taught when I saw father leap overboard. I shut down the engine and just as he disappeared I saw that the rope was wound around one of his shins. So I dived in after him and I cut the rope, but not before it had put a deep groove in his leg. "What was all that in aid of?" I said, fishing him out of the water.

"I saw right at the last minute I was standing in the coil of rope, I had to go overboard with it, otherwise the rope would have broken my leg or something equally as serious." "So better to have a broken leg and drown, than just have a broken leg?" I mocked.
"I didn't have that long to think," he snarled.

I turned the boat around and explained to the people on the marooned yacht that I had to get father to hospital, but I was willing to tow them off before I went. One of the ladies was crying and one of the men had untied our rope and handed it to me, saying they would prefer to wait for the tide. Who could blame them?

The outcome at the hospital was father would make a full recovery in a few weeks. Once we got home and mother had stopped crying, I did my disappearing act to the lake. The leaves were falling, making the whole place more open, but not so inviting after all the different warm colours of summer. I made my way to the swimming pool. The pump had been switched off, which meant the water was no longer being chlorinated or filtered, turning it into a foreboding dark green with a cover put over the top of the pool and the water left un-drained. This way any small animal that fell in could escape, that's how it was till the following May.

The girls were returning from the summer break and I was old and strong enough to help father with the trunks that needed hauling out of cars and into dormitories. I volunteered to do any work at the school for the chance of seeing Jennifer, no luck. Instead I came face to face with Miss Joyce, the headmistress.

"George I've been meaning to have a word with you, would you be kind enough to knock on my study door when you have finished?"

"That could be after midnight," I said.

"I will still receive you," she said, followed by her usual distinct "hmmmmm" as she walked away. I always wondered if that was her way of showing her disapproval of me loitering around the school, till Jennifer explained to me that she always ended a conversation on that note.

It was indeed after mid-night when I tentatively knocked on her door. "Come in George," she said. As I entered the room she stood up from her desk which was illuminated by a small antique lamp, the walls were stained oak panelling. I imagined a secret door somewhere, a priest hole perhaps.

She gestured towards some easy chairs that were by an unlit fireplace. ""Take a seat and stop looking so nervous. George it is my responsibility to know all that goes on in the school. We did have a family who looked after the grounds the same as your father does, before it became a school, they had a boy who grew up here, I am therefore use to having a young male about the place. He fell in love with all the girls here and it was not seen as a problem, he could hardly take them all home to meet mother, if you see what I mean."

I felt co-incidentally that she must have been talking about the guy I met at the lake.

"Oh heck", I thought. Is she going to tell me not to come to the school anymore. She continued. "You on the other hand have a singular interest; you are very fond of a girl called Jennifer. I want you to realise that when the girls finish here they will leave and forget you, and you will be left with your feelings in tatters. The last person I need at the school is an embittered young man and I want you to realise this before it happens. I'm not going to stop you from seeing the girls. As long as it doesn't interfere with their work, you may pass the time of day with them." "She hasn't returned yet?" I said.
"No she hasn't. I wondered why you were so eager to help your father tonight."
Blimey, I thought, the old girl doesn't miss a trick.
"I've been told she has had an exhausting summer break and needs some rest. She will not be back until the beginning of October, why don't you take the time she is not here to imagine the place without her, and to find a way of coming to terms with it. Goodnight George."

The weeks passed by and I realised Miss Joyce was right, when I looked at the school and the grounds, all I saw was Jenny. I was mulling all this over at my usual place of safety; the lake. I hadn't noticed but it was getting dark, I had not heard the footsteps but the voice was as clear as crystal. "What's the matter, cat got your tongue?"

"Who's there?" I asked.

"Who do you think; you haven't got an army of admirers you know."

"Jenny, what are you doing here?"

"I can always go."

"No, I meant I wasn't expecting you and its dark, how did you know I was here?" "Miss Joyce isn't the only person who knows everything."

"Don't talk to me about her, although to be fair she gave me some motherly advice and it's brought me down to earth with a bang."

"I know, I heard."

"What do you mean you've heard? I haven't told anyone"

"Oh let's just say the walls have ears."

"No," I said. "Let's not say the walls have ears."

"Oh come on don't lets fight. Walk me back to the school, the bedtime bell went ages ago."

I went to place a great big kiss on her lips but she backed away saying. ""Ah ah, don't be greedy." Then she ran off. I chased her all the way back to the school, by the time I had reached the first block of classrooms I was fighting for breath with my head bent towards my knees, when I straightened up she had gone. All the good advice Miss Joyce had given me disappeared that night. In its place came a rush of love I had for Jenny, I really could not think logically, but that's what happens when love comes calling.

It was a dismal wet Saturday night when there was a knock at the front door. No one should be out on a night like this one; it was an evening only for burying oneself in a good book. No one else would move so I answered the door. There stood a man in his mid twenties, black curly hair, black leather jacket and jeans; he towered over me by at least a couple of feet.

"You must be George?" he said. "I'm Mike, is Karen in?"

"Wait there, I'll have a look."

Before I could open my mouth Karen told me to get rid of him.

"Sort out your own problems," I said.

"I'll go," said father. I could make out a very lengthy conversation with the odd "But I love her" thrown in, and father's boring drawl as he tried to extricate this man from our threshold.

I heard the man sobbing. "You're really hard Karen—he seems such a nice bloke."

"Well you go out with him then."

"Why couldn't you tell him it's over?"

"I have till I'm blue in the face, he just won't accept it."

"Well if this is how you treat blokes I'm glad I'm your brother and not your boyfriend."

"Look," said Karen. "You have found the love of your life and I'm very pleased for you, but don't get carried away. You've been lucky, for some of us romance is a bit harder to find, just remember that before you get too much of a smug grin on your face."

"I'll have to give him some tips on how my sister likes to be treated."

"You will do no such thing, he's messed things up well enough on his own he doesn't need your help."

Half-term came which meant we were going for a week's camp to Cornwall. Father wanted to take me night-fishing near some rocks he knew. I was looking forward to this holiday as the sun was shining all the way, which gave us all a lift. It wasn't till we were pitching the tent that the rain decided to lash down drenching everything. Another hour and all would have been well, no fishing for us tonight just a change of clothes and an early night.

The following evening we made off for the rocks. You had to be a mountain goat just to negotiate the footpath but we were soon enjoying catching loads of fish, mostly sea bream.

It was quite dark when we decided to pack up, mainly because it had started to rain heavily again—and I then heard the sound of Amanda's violin. I wondered what was in store for me on this desolate rocky headland, with no way of getting help should the worse happen.

We turned to leave and noticed the white horses crashing over the rocks, we were cut off and the only escape was through waist high water and an eighty-foot climb up the cliffs. With the thought of one slip will be the last we climbed the cliff with rods and tackle with the rain preventing any clear visibility of where the next hand hold would be.

As I got to the top I stumble backwards, the fall was eighty feet back onto the rocks but I noticed a gorse bush at the last second, my only hope. I knew the thorns would tear open the palms of my hands. If I couldn't stand the pain, then the fall would kill me. As I grabbed hold of a handful of gorse I couldn't believe my luck, some pieces of cloth had snagged on the thorns just where I took hold of it and I pulled myself to safety.

Father came over to me. He thought I was a goner. I told him what had happened and he examined the material. "This is green felt."

"Is it?" I said without showing any interest, he continued. "This is the same type of material used to make the blazers and the berets for the girls at Farthings, would you believe it."

When we arrived back at the tent the ridge pole had snapped due to the excessive wind and rain. Mother was trying to hold everything together, whilst my sisters were moaning that their hair was getting wet. In the middle of all this, mother chose to announce she was pregnant, causing all of us to change our attitudes and give her a hand. Meanwhile what we caught on the rocks that night kept us in fish for the whole week. Lovely.

CHAPTER 9

By the time we arrived back at Farthings the girls had returned from half-term. There was a buzz of excitement about the place, a lot more than usual I would say; just as unusual was that father was called in to see Miss Joyce.

When he arrived home he told us that Miss Joyce had hired the services of a medium. There was a ghost, possibly ghosts, at the school and it was disrupting the girls' concentration. I decided to go to my usual place, the lake, once there it didn't take long before the love of my life appeared. She was asking some very forward questions—how much did I love her, how far would I go to protect her? I hadn't expected any of this after what Miss Joyce had lectured me on. However I took the opportunity to tell her I would die for her—that was the depth of my love.

That Friday father received a letter in the post, its contents caused him and mother to talk behind closed doors. I caught snippets of conversation. "I like it here." "Yes but we are from the coast, the kids love the sea." I put two and two together and could not wait to find Jennifer to let her know I was probably on the move; what was I going to do?

I found her by the swimming pool. I explained the situation; she reassured me that everything would be all right. We planned to meet at the lake that evening to talk some more.

It was eight o'clock and getting dark. I thought Jennifer would never appear and was about to go home when I heard her call to me. I looked around but couldn't see her. She called once more; and then I could see she was in the rowing boat in the middle of the lake.

"Wait there I will come and get you," she said. After a short time she pulled up alongside the bank and I stepped into the boat and she rowed us out to the middle.
"What's this all about?" I said.
"You'll see," she giggled.
She seemed to be looking for a particular place on the lake to stop the boat. When she found it she shipped the oars and stood up. I said: "Careful you will have us both in the water."

"Stand up with me and give me a kiss will you?" Now an invitation to kiss Jennifer with a risk of falling into the water or not was a temptation I could not resist. As our mouths were about to meet, she told me to close my eyes and said. "You're going nowhere."

The next thing I knew I was falling into the lake and everything went black.

* * *

No one slept very much that night. The study room of Miss Joyce, once a peaceful room, was now filled with Police, my father, a priest, Miss Joyce and Mr Foresight the medium.

My father broke the silence. "Can you shed any light on my son's death?" He asked Miss Joyce.

"Yes," she said. "I had the ghost of Commander Rubens right here in this room. Mr Foresight told me who it was; luckily he was here at the time."

"I can confirm that," said Mr Foresight interrupting.

Miss Joyce continued. "He was shouting out, 'Find George. Stop George going to the lake.' I sent a prefect to your house, she got no response—you were all out. I phoned the Police, but by the time I had convinced them that I wasn't mad and they had arrived it was all too late."

Inspector Fairbrass said: "The Police divers said she took him to the bottom, in the deepest part of the lake, they will never recover his body."

"Does anybody know anything about this girl?" asked father.

"Only that she was the granddaughter of Commander Rubens, her name is Jennifer, and her and all her family were drowned in a boating accident years ago", said Mr Foresight.

"Can we trace her through her surname, does anyone know it?" asked father. "No," said Mr Foresight. "The only person who would have known that would have been George, and well, he's no longer with us."

"How about you Miss Joyce can you help?" asked father.

"No," she said, "I only enrol the living."

"But you gave George some advice on a girl called Jennifer," said father, "he told me as much."

"Yes," she said. "I thought it was Jennifer Whimlock, who is a very attractive girl. I would hardly have given George advice on a ghost, really."

Can you contact George, Mr Foresight?" said father.

"No, they have both passed over."

"How about Commander Rubens?"

"No, there are no more ghosts here at Farthings."

"Why was her ghost here, can you help us on that Mr Foresight?"

"Yes", he said, "she was born a short while after George, they had a special bond between them, her ghost has been looking after George ever since your family moved here, that's why she came to Farthings, she recognised the name as the same name from Portsmouth. She couldn't pass over without taking George with her. As soon as she was convinced their special bond had not been broken she took him."

"But why tonight, of all nights?"

"You received a letter this morning which meant your family might be moving away, so she had to take him tonight before he left."

"So", said father, "she didn't come here to trace Commander Rubens?"

"No", said Mr Foresight, "Commander Rubens would have liked that and he had the school built for her, so if she did appear she would have girls as company, even bringing the name Farthings with him to help guide her here. But no, she came for George. As soon as she knew his family were here she appeared, the lake was a bonus."

He continued. "George always thought that Amanda was his guardian angel, as he heard violin music that warned him of danger. The sound the violin made was unique to Amanda, as she had the only one in the country."

"Was she a ghost as well?" asked father.

"No," said Mr Foresight. "Jennifer's father was in the navy, he brought the same violin back from America. George and Jennifer loved to sit and listen, while he played it. Their bond was so close that most times the violin was the only way both of them would go to sleep at night.

"It's my entire fault," said father. "I came here to trace Commander Rubens. I saw the name Farthings as well. If I hadn't come here she would never have found us and George would still be alive."

"Well that's hindsight, and possibly not true," said Miss Joyce. "Now if you will all excuse me I have a school full of hysterical girls to calm down. I'll see if the dear priest has finished his tea; some of the girls may need his help. I will be up till the early hours talking to them in the gym."

The following day the priest, who had been up all night, held a service at the lakeside. All the girls were there along with the Sea Cadet Corps who had been invited to attend, they were using their boats to take girls onto the lake to enable them to place their wreaths and flowers on the spot where George had disappeared. Amanda and Natasha seemed to have the largest wreath and they were certainly crying most bitterly.

The school secretary had managed to contact Joan Edenbridge who was comforting mother along with Abi and Karen, who were still in a state of shock that they had lost their brother in circumstances where he seemed at his happiest. Miss Joyce had decided the school rowing boat would be a permanent fixture on the lake in memory of George, as there would not be a grave. Father agreed and asked Miss Joyce to include Jennifer on the plaque as George loved her with all his heart no matter what form she appeared in.

At the end of the service as everyone was walking away, father caught up with the Headmistress. "Miss Joyce," said father, "I have been contacted by the owner of Commander Ruben's old house at Farthings near Portsmouth."

"And you want to leave?" She asked.

"Yes," said father. "We cannot stay here under the circumstances, and my wife is expecting."

"Of course," she commented. "I do understand. What are you hoping for?"

"She has had a scan; we are having a boy next spring. The family who have taken over Commander Rubens house, well the wife is expecting; she is having a girl about the same time."

"Congratulations," replied Miss Joyce. "I shall forward references to your new employer; you have nothing to worry about. I will be sad to see you go. Do you know much about him?"

"Not much except that he married Commander Ruben's youngest daughter. The house should have been passed down to the Commander's eldest daughter, but she and her family all died in a boating accident years ago."

"I know the address from the files, do you have his name?"

"Yes," said father, "Rear Admiral, I can't think straight I've been up all night, oh! I have his letter in my pocket. Here it is, Rear Admiral Sir John Bradley."

THE END